CONSIGNMENT

This book is a work of fiction.

All characters and events are the products of the author's imagination.

The story is part of a series but stands alone.

Series Titles

WHITE COLLAR OPTION

THEN GO STRAIGHT FORWARD

WAITING FOR THE STORM TO PASS

THEIR WILL BE DONE

POINTED INWARDS

MADE TO ACCOUNT

CHAIN REACTION

CONSIGNMENT

The author has been a journalist for more than 30 years; among the many news outlets for which he has worked are The Times, Observer, the BBC and UPI. He has taught journalism in the UK and USA.

He was born in Glasgow, Scotland but lived for many years in London and Washington, DC where much of this story is located.

Many thanks to family and friends for their support which made this book possible.

Special thanks to Rosamund for her support, encouragement, patience and diligent proofreading.

Additional thanks to Di and Ian Cormack, also Steve Murray and Bob Meek, whose critical eyes help spot the errors which may have got away.

Thanks to my pal Barney for keeping me company while I searched for the words.

writegoodenglish.wix.com/billjohnstonenovels

PREFACE

The creak of knee-high leather boots carried across the empty cobble-stoned courtyard as the guards patrolled inside the perimeter fence. Barbed wire twirled its way, like a menacing helix, along the top of the electrified boundary beneath the spotlights in the shadows of the machine-gun turrets. The guards in the two towers, which flanked the entrance, watched the soldiers below. None had any idea what lay ahead.

One of the two guards on the tower, to the left of the gate, felt a sharp pain in the small of his back, tried to shout but was muffled by the hand over his mouth, as his knees buckled and he silently slid to the floor. His companion, his back half-turned as he lit a cigarette, felt a similar sharp deadly pain as he too fell on his face. Both guards, now slumped in a bundle on the top of the tower, were unable to see the same thing happening on the other, to the right of the gate. Within seconds, the guards there too were dead, heaped into the centre of their tower, in silence.

The driver of the truck which had pulled up outside the compound waited for the guard at the gate to approach. On request the driver reached for his credentials in the glove compartment, but instead pulled out an automatic with a fitted silencer and fired. The hiss of a bullet, a sound barely detectable, smashed into the forehead of the surprised guard. He dropped to the ground with barely a sound. By the time his partner on the other side of the gate had noticed, he'd suffered the same fate. A figure quickly jumped from the truck which drove swiftly through the now open gate to the building in the centre of the compound. Six soldiers in commando fatigues dropped instantly from the vehicle. They knew what to do. They would deal with any other resistance.

Within minutes they'd broken into the unit and, after another ten, had taken what they wanted, now packed into a specially designed mobile container they'd brought with them. Seconds later, loaded onto the truck, it was on its way from this remote site in Soviet Georgia, via a waiting jet, to a predetermined destination. There it would be met by another armed escort which would chaperone the deadly cargo.

CHAPTER 1

 The cool air in the metro was a relief from the stifling humidity outside. An early Washington summer had arrived and with it the predictable steamy weather. It was impossible to get comfortable anywhere except inside where the mercies of air conditioning excelled. McCabe felt the phone vibrate in the breast pocket of his damp and sticky shirt. It was a text from the newsdesk. He pushed the phone forward slightly to read it. The message was stark, brutally frank, devoid of subtlety or even accompanied by any sentiment. '*Andy Gallagher died this morning at his home in Scotland. Cause unknown.*'

McCabe slipped slowly onto a vacant seat, his mind a jumble of images, incidents, and scenes about the man who had been his mentor, who had taught him everything he knew, whose style had left an indelible imprint on his life.

 It was difficult to imagine a world without Andy Gallagher. Somehow, with his charming persona and his penetrating tenacious intelligence, one expected him to be around forever.

 McCabe was stunned by the news. It had been more than ten years since he had seen him and several decades since they'd worked together. But somehow those times felt like yesterday, vivid and vibrant images that were as real as if they were taking place now. He allowed himself the slightest of smiles, an immediate monument to the man who had given him so much.

He got off at *Metro Center* in the heart of Washington then climbed the stairs on the escalator two at a time. At the top, breathless, he punched his cell phone. 'McCabe,' he said, still out of breath. 'What do you know? Tell me!'

He leaned against the wall opposite the escalator, trying to pick a spot which wasn't in the way of the commuter torrent pouring from the stairs. He was still dodging the onslaught when he got a reply. He switched ears, hoping he'd get a better signal, but it was still difficult to decipher the fading voice.

'We don't have any details Mike. Some sort of car crash. They called through from London a few minutes ago. I know he was close to you. Thought you'd like to know immediately. He was killed instantly, not far from his home in Glasgow. Apparently, he'd just come off a flight from the US. I was asked to contact you. That's all I know.'

'Was it an accident?' McCabe asked quickly. He could hear the clatter of an office in the background, as he waited for an answer. Even in the world of computers and electronics, far from the mayhem of clanking manual typewriters, there seemed to be an irritating buzz that was always present.

'I'm just checking the file, Mike. There's nothing more. That's it, sorry!'

McCabe held the phone close to him in silence for a moment. He didn't make a move. He looked like some human sculpture which had been dumped on the sidewalk. Pictures of Gallagher's face flashed in front of him. He could hear his distinctive voice echo in the silence. Suddenly he murmured down the phone,

'Thanks!' It was barely audible. 'Thanks,' he repeated slowly. 'I'll get back to you.'

Within five minutes he'd pressed the elevator button in the Press Building two blocks away. The light for the thirteenth floor for the Press Club flashed below his index finger. Every time he saw that number flash, he felt he was defying a superstition, one that inhibited the rest of humanity. Perhaps that's what it was supposed to do? Was that not what his profession was meant to do, challenge the status quo? He slipped out of the empty elevator, made his way to the lounge and helped himself to the member's free buffet breakfast. He didn't remember selecting the coffee, bagels and fruit. But they appeared. He was on automatic pilot.

McCabe took a small table at the far end of the room, away from the groups chatting in the centre. The breakfast hadn't distracted him. He was still thinking of Andy Gallagher. He could see him vividly again, the images as clear as if he was in real time. He could picture him leaning over his old manual typewriter, peering at the text he'd just written. Not for the first time had he heard him swear at the top of his voice and then watched as he ripped out the paper, crumpled it into a ball and as he clenched his teeth, threw it with amazing accuracy into the middle of the wastebin at the far end of the room. At the same time, he would lean across to the end of the desk, pick up the cigarette that had been slowly burning in the ashtray and salvage the last of it before he quickly lit another.

McCabe sighed, as if he'd just acknowledged the passing of an era. There was no doubt it had and the man he would now mourn was its architect. He finished the breakfast then phoned the newsdesk in London; no more details. Fifteen minutes later, in the Washington office, he checked his laptop; still no details.

Now Editor-at-Large for the *London Daily Herald*, based in the US capital, he was a long way from the life he had shared with Gallagher on a local weekly newspaper just outside London. They'd lost touch when Gallagher returned to his native Glasgow and McCabe moved on to the international stage, reporting on every human tragedy, from dozens of exotic locations around the globe, a far cry from the days when he'd written about weddings, funerals and the banality of local council meetings.

He hadn't forgotten any of it and the lessons he'd drawn from the experience. *The story within the story* was the bedrock on which his career had been founded, taught to him by Gallagher.

However, what he was sure of was that unless this old warhorse had changed, Andy Gallagher was likely to be chasing some tale or other. To him, news stories were as vital to his existence as the blood which pumped through his Gaelic veins. McCabe, he was to find, was made from the same mould.

CHAPTER 2

As he tightened his seatbelt, the announcement from the pilot said they were about to make their final approach and would be on the ground in Glasgow in less than half an hour. McCabe would have the day ahead of him; one advantage of the early morning flight via New York. But it was going to be a long one.

Once out of customs he picked up his rental, took a lungful of the fresh Scottish air, which he hadn't sampled for a long time, and tried to adjust to the new time zone. He'd forgotten how pleasant summers could be outside the sticky US capital. It was cool and there was a slight breeze and no humidity.

He drove the short distance to the city centre and checked into his hotel. A shower and a change of clothes and he would be good to go. It had been a week since he'd heard the news of Andy Gallagher. In that time, he'd barely stopped thinking about him. He looked at his watch. It was time.

McCabe pulled into the cemetery on the northside of Glasgow. The cold nip in the air hit him as he opened the car door. He pulled his jacket collar up under his chin but he could feel his cheeks tingling. He'd forgotten that the mornings could take a sharp turn, particularly on open ground. Such was the unpredictable character of this Scottish weather.

He'd arrived just in time to catch the start of the funeral service; no embarrassing and tedious wait. Mercifully, the service was short; no laboured prayers or torturous predictable eulogy delivered by a locum minister whom Andy would probably have never known.

McCabe, seated at the back of the church, was last to leave giving him a chance to scan the faces as the crowd made its way out. He didn't recognise anyone. The small line of mourners filed out of the church towards the graveside while a group belonging to the next funeral hovered outside, waiting to fill the void.

He followed the procession to the graveside, took part in more prayers and, relieved, slipped quietly towards the cemetery exit. He would have liked to have said a few words about his friend but there was no opportunity. Everything now seemed to move slowly along with a momentum all of its own. He walked towards his car, occasionally looking back to see if he still might recognise a face or two.

'You're McCabe?' said a distinctive Glaswegian gravelled voice behind him.

McCabe turned slowly to face its owner, a big man by any measure, who'd surely been a rugby prop forward at some stage in his career or a very effective stop for something.

'Wullie O'Neill,' the man said, sticking out his right hand, the size of a shovel. There was nothing flabby about the greeting that followed. He had hands that could have crushed walnuts with little effort.

McCabe could feel his hand tighten as he watched it disappear into O'Neill's huge grip. He remembered writing an article, years before, headlined, *In Defence of the Irish Navy*. It was a fascinating piece. Apparently, the name came from a shortened version of navigational engineers, describing the labourers who built the canals and railways in Britain nearly two hundred years ago and later the same in America. The predominance of workers from Ireland made the name stick. O'Neill's huge frame and hands reminded him of the hardworking and equally hard-drinking men he'd met while writing the article in Britain and the USA; a truly remarkable experience.

'I knew Andy Gallagher. They don't come any finer,' O'Neill said, his eyes following a black BMW which had just entered the cemetery and drew up beside the church a few hundred yards away.

'Do I know you?'

'I'm head of what you would probably call homicide, for the Glasgow police. Murder squad, in simple local parlance,' said O'Neill.

'Murder?'

'We get roped in if there's an unexplained death,' he said quickly.

'I didn't know it was unexplained,' replied McCabe cautiously. 'I'm getting confusing stories about what actually happened,' he added quietly, as if he didn't want to be overheard. He looked towards the graveside, at the far end of the cemetery, at the last trickle of mourners making their way to the parked cars.

'You mean the crash?' asked the policeman as he too now stared at the mourners and then to the duo who had got out of the

BMW and were walking to the far end of the cemetery. He didn't say anything for a moment.

McCabe nodded. 'Yes; the crash.'

O'Neill drew lightly on a roll-up cigarette then turned his attention back to McCabe. 'What's to know? The car went out of control and he hit a wall at the side of the road. It was curtains, instant, fucking dead,' he said delivering the words as if they had been rehearsed, almost scripted. But it was a poor performance; no Oscar for delivery or conviction.

'You don't sound too persuasive,' said McCabe, watching the detective carefully for a reaction, anything that would give him some indication of how he really felt.

But the policeman's face was deadpan, a poker player's face, difficult to read.

Again he said nothing for a moment then nodded towards the two men now standing back beside the BMW. His stoic expression still gave nothing away, as he stared. But it was soon obvious there was something bubbling beneath the surface; he was fighting an inside force that eventually he couldn't contain. 'It's not my story. It's theirs.' He seemed to spit the words in the direction of the BMW.

McCabe watched as the detective stood rigid, still staring at the figures about a hundred yards away.

'Theirs,' he repeated. 'Not mine; theirs.' His emphasis said it all. The policeman's disapproval was hardly disguised. He stood pointing his huge right hand in the direction of the BMW and shaking his head.

McCabe knew there were many times when the follow-up question had to be carefully timed. This was certainly one; this man was angry. He hoped an answer would surface without prompting, The reason for the detective's animosity would soon become apparent. There was no need to push him. McCabe would take it a step at a time and small ones at that. 'Didn't your guys examine the wreckage?' he asked quietly.

O'Neill turned back towards McCabe and shook his head slightly from side to side. 'No, we didn't.' This policeman was not a happy bunny. 'Interfering bastards,' he said in a voice that was far from a whisper. It was intended to be heard. 'It's obvious that he wasn't chasing a pot of gold. That didn't interest Andy. For him it was always the story. Which leaves the obvious question; what was it?' He walked away then turned back. He looked really unsettled. 'Interfering bastards,' he repeated. 'They impounded it; the car.'

'Impounded?' queried McCabe. 'What does that mean?'

'You're a journalist, McCabe. Don't fuck with me. You know what that means.'

Before McCabe could respond, the detective raved again. He was on a roll. 'They stole it, McCabe. That's what it means. Before anybody could blink an eye; they stole it. They took it, so no one else could inspect it.' He stopped for a moment, finished the last of his cigarette then flicked it on the ground in front of him. Something was eating this big man. 'What had Andy to do with those kinds of people, anyway?' he asked, turning back to the figures beside the BMW 'What in God's name was he doing dealing with these guys?'

McCabe followed his gaze towards the car again. 'Who are they?' he asked quietly, not wishing to create any unnecessary waves.

'You may well ask.' He pulled another roll-up from a battered tobacco tin in his pocket. 'I did,' he said, sounding frustrated. 'I didn't get a straight answer; neither would you. It doesn't take much to work out.'

'You're losing me again, detective.'

O'Neill lit his new roll-up then glared at him. 'They produced all sorts of fancy credentials. National Security they call it. You can drive a carthorse through that gate without much explanation these days.'

McCabe was getting the picture, albeit a small piece at a time. Certainly Andy Gallagher could tackle any story and the detective was right; that's what drove him. You could give him a million dollars but it wouldn't interest him. But the story behind making it would be what would fire him.

'Spooks, they're spooks.' O'Neill spat the words out again with obvious venom. 'What was Andy doing with the likes of them?' He sounded like a despairing father. He turned towards the exit.

McCabe touched the detective lightly on a sleeve. 'I feel as if I've missed a few chapters in this story. '

'You're not the only one, McCabe. But they haven't left my manor yet,' O'Neill said glancing towards the BMW again. There was a threat, if not a promise, in the words.

'Why would you think Andy was in any way involved with these people?' asked McCabe.

'They're at his funeral, aren't they?'

'Out to see who has an interest. Just like you?' replied McCabe, cautiously.

O'Neill drew heavily on his roll-up. He ignored the comment. 'This is my manor. I know what goes on, who comes in and who goes out, what the good guys do and what the villains are up to. When that pattern changes, I can tell, it's instinctive.'

McCabe thought the case overstated and the detective's response perhaps a little exaggerated. But he did have a point. 'Where does Andy fit into this, do you think?'

O'Neill shook his head. 'For once, I don't know. But they've prevented us from examining the car. What does that tell you?'

McCabe was ready to mouth some sort of answer.

The question wasn't meant to be rhetorical. The detective beat him to a response. 'They were interested in something he did or knew. I can tell you these guys are not chasing unpaid parking fines. They're playing for bigger stakes. You don't need to be an ace journalist or detective to work that out, do you?'

'You'll need to spell that out for me,' said McCabe, being intentionally obtuse.

'You'll just have to work that out for yourself. You knew Andy as well as I did.'

It was obvious O'Neill wasn't going to let it rest. He flicked his second roll-up onto the ground. 'I know you'll be asking a few question, McCabe. I want some answers too. If you need any help, you know where to find me,' he said handing McCabe a business card. 'Be careful. This doesn't smell right to me.'

But it was evident that O'Neill wouldn't be drawn further.

The policeman never added anything more. He opened his huge hands, shrugged his shoulders then walked away. He turned as he got to the exit, looked at the figures who'd got back into the BMW then glanced at McCabe again. Then he was gone.

McCabe followed him out of the exit to the car park, slid into the driving seat of his car quickly and started it up. There had been the customary invitation at the graveside to join the party to toast or celebrate the deceased at the local hotel. He'd decided to give it a miss. But before he'd got the car into gear, there was a slight tap on the window. A small man smiled and waved at him through the glass.

'Can I help you,' said McCabe winding down the window. He didn't recognise the figure but he had seen him at the ceremony.

'I didn't expect to see you here,' said the man. 'Not quite the state occasions you're probably used to now eh, Mike? Andy would have been glad to see you here. I'm sure. '

McCabe was flattered but a little bemused. Who was this man, he hadn't the slightest idea?

'You'll be coming back for a wee dram, Mike?'

McCabe studied the face for some clue; but nothing.

'You've got a bit older but you've still got the fine features.' He looked at McCabe's hair. 'And not too much grey there either.'

He laughed.

'Good living,' said McCabe with a smile. The line wasn't meant to be convincing. 'How are you? Good to see you,' he said, not sounding too confident.

The old man laughed a little. 'You don't know who I am, do you? No reason why you should. Time has taken its toll, so has life.' He laughed again. 'You probably remember my wife Sadie more than me?'

McCabe's face lit up. Sadie Smith was the departmental secretary in Gallagher's local newspaper and was a wonderful human being. She was always there for McCabe when he tripped. In those days that happened frequently, as he fumbled his way as a cub reporter, learning what he could about the job and the things that life invariably threw at him.

'Gus Smith,' the man said quietly and extended his right hand. McCabe looked about. 'I'd love to see Sadie again. How is she? Is she here with you?' he asked looking around.

Smith face lost its smile. 'Three years ago, she was taken. It was quite unexpected; very sudden. She didn't suffer,' he said taking his cap off. He said no more then put his cap back on.

'I'm sorry,' McCabe mumbled. The words sounded totally inadequate and trite. He was told they were rarely seen outside the office without each other.

Gus Smith sighed a little. 'I miss her. I suppose someone had to go first. My bad luck it was her.' He started to walk away. McCabe wanted to ask him about Andy Gallagher but now seemed the wrong time and place. 'I was shocked by the news of Andy's accident.'

Smith didn't respond, except with a slight shake of his head. 'I might see you later, then? Have a drink for Andy.'

McCabe felt a little awkward. 'I won't manage the reception,' he said. 'But I wanted to ask you about Andy but it probably isn't the.... ' The words seemed to disappear, as Gus Smith continued to walk away.

'I didn't see him that often, after he moved back to Glasgow from London. He was supposed to be retired but he still filed the odd story or two to the nationals. I know he'd been in America recently.'

'What was he doing there?'

Smith shrugged his shoulders. 'I wouldn't know the answer to that. However, unless the leopard has changed his spots he was working on some story or other.' He laughed again.

'Irene, you couldn't have forgotten her I'm sure? She's the only family he had left. She was at the funeral but you would hardly recognise her now, I suppose?'

McCabe certainly hadn't forgotten her, although it had been more than twenty years since he'd seen her; Irene Campbell, her uncle's pride and joy.

'They do well for themselves, they do well for you,' he remembered Andy saying to him. His joy, Irene, was a babe in arms then.

'I'm going for a dram, anyway. Nice to have seen you again,' Smith said as he shuffled away. 'You're looking well.' He stopped for a moment and looked back at McCabe. 'Irene will tell you more about Andy. As I said, I've been a bit out of touch.

She's probably staying at the old place. You remember that, I'm sure?'

Somehow McCabe felt as if a whole world walked away with him. He wanted to say something that was meaningful, anything that told this lonely figure how much his late wife had meant to everyone who knew her. But he didn't. He just stared after the old man as he walked slowly out of the gate.

CHAPTER 3

Andrei Krupin looked out over the lawn that flanked the Russian Embassy in Washington, DC as the light rain drizzled onto the grass and gently sprayed the cars in the driveway. The few flowers in the garden now looked a little limp and sodden.

He still wasn't sure if he liked Washington. It was a pretty city, certainly, and the hub of US politics, a quagmire of world diplomatic jousting. Perhaps that is what made him uncomfortable, uncertain about his feelings. So different from the world he had left. He was told some people survived the cultural transition, others never made it. In the other places he'd operated in, the diplomatic code was full of innuendos and half-meanings, a stark contrast to the American culture which was much more candid.

He turned away from the window towards the desk in the middle of the room. The intelligence reports lying across it, which he'd just finishing examining, were scanty and told him nothing. They had agents in several countries investigating what had happened but there was no clear picture and the conclusions that they had arrived at were worthless, if not contradictory. He returned to his desk and leafed through one report in particular. He read it twice, thumped his hand on the desk in frustration then read it again. Why was it so vague and why did it involve him? He knew the answer to both questions which gave him little satisfaction. When their agents had no information on this type of issue the buck stopped at Washington. That is where the answers would be found, so he was told. He was furious at the assumption. A knock on the door was followed by a head appearing cautiously from behind. 'Sir, you wanted to see me?' asked the striking and elegantly dressed female aide, speaking without the slightest trace of a Russian accent.

Three years in two of New England's best universities had taken more than the rough edges off her delivery and in any company she would command attention. She looked at her watch and then at the clock on the wall beside the windows. 'We have a meeting scheduled. Is that still on?'

Hanya Smolka, blonde and tall, was a linguist of remarkable talent, initially recruited by Russian security with a brief that was surprisingly liberal. In theory she was a diplomat, a trade attaché and a liaison officer between the Embassy and the outside world. She was a patriot, and there were few who would doubt her sincerity in that regard, but some hardliners would call her *Americanised* and too sympathetic to some western ideals. She was in that limbo which they considered dangerous. They didn't like the imbalance. Her response to such criticism was robust, defending her stance as that of a professional, which required her to be familiar with the values and the cultural priorities of Russia's enemies. She insisted on speaking English, even in the Embassy.

Krupin had been well briefed about her before taking up his post. There seemed to be a divided opinion among his contacts in Moscow about her. She was well connected, known to many members of the politburo, but it wasn't just the hardliners who had reservations about her loyalty. While most applauded her ability to assimilate easily American culture, some distrusted her and considered her a risk. They also knew she was being watched by US Intelligence who had ambitions to recruit her. When the US idea had been disclosed to her by her superiors, she laughed. They laughed with her but didn't easily dismiss the proposition. That the Americans considered her a prospect was enough to make them wary.

Krupin pointed to the chair in front of the desk and nodded towards the seat. 'Do sit down Hanya. I've been reading what our intelligence people call a report on this Georgia incident. It tells me nothing; absolutely nothing. Do forgive me if I have to resort to our own beloved language. I know you like to show off your excellent English,' he said sounding a little patronising.

'Of course, comrade,' she said, formally.

'Have you read this?' he asked pushing the folder forward on his desk.

She could read the label quite clearly from where she was seated. She agreed with Krupin. It hadn't told her much either but it painted a picture, one that left her with a dozen questions. The raid had taken place and the materials removed, apparently with military precision. That was as much as they knew. 'Yes, I have,' she said, nodding slightly and waiting for Krupin to make a comment.

He pulled back the folder, opened it, leafed through the few pages it contained, closed it then stared straight at her. 'There seems to be a number of interested parties.' He stopped for a moment. 'The Americans and the British are already involved.' She stared back at him, waiting for the punchline. Why was he talking to her about this? For some curious reason, which she couldn't understand, it seemed to involve her.

Krupin opened the drawer to his left and pulled out another folder, read it slowly, clearly for effect. It was meant to be dramatic and make her feel uneasy.

She was fighting her desire to laugh. They were amateur theatrics which looked as if they'd been lifted from a very old copy of a KGB interview manual. Undoubtedly the folder was the latest report on her progress. She had only recently returned to the US, after a long spell in China.

He turned to what was the last page, gave another dramatic sigh and then looked at her.

She didn't have the slightest hint of what was coming.

'Mike McCabe,' he said without inflection.

The words tested all her training. She didn't flinch.

Krupin looked disappointed. It was obvious he expected a reaction.

But Hanya Smolka, professional, could play those games too.

'Sorry, was that meant to be a question?' she asked coolly.

He seemed thrown, initially, but recovered quickly. He flipped back through a few of the top sheets of the folder, read one, fingered it and moved it to one side. He read the one below it then looked up. 'Mike McCabe, British journalist, He now has quite a reputation. He's moved on since you met him last.'

She detected another attempt at the dramatic, in an effort to make her feel uncomfortable; a frustrated actor looking for applause, she thought. So McCabe had done well; good luck to him. It didn't surprise her that he would. The drive and ambition he'd shown long ago as a naive young man had not gone without reward. She would have loved to air her feelings now but that was more than her status would allow. Her face showed no emotion.

Krupin looked uncomfortable. She had obviously not taken the bait. 'You haven't seen him since that time in Moscow,' he said quickly.

Another question, she sensed, delivered as a statement. This game was going to get tedious. It was already. She still said nothing and stared blankly at him. There was no other way to respond to this banality. In time, he'd have to show his hand.

'You don't remember?' he asked, sounding surprised. 'Or do you just prefer to keep your private life a secret? You should know that in our business, we have no personal secrets?'

She knew he had none to speak of. His wife had run off with a young army officer. There was no one who didn't know about it and few who were sympathetic. She would not rejoice in his misfortune but she was struggling to show him any charity. He was loathed by his colleagues and she found it hard to hold a different view.

'Sir,' she said very slowly. 'If you could be a little more precise, I might be able to help. What is it you are asking? What is it you want from me?' She delivered her lines, almost staccato, emotionless, as if reading from a script.

Her formality appeared to throw him.

His rhythm now seemed a little stilted. He hesitated and stuttered a response. 'He's likely to be involved,' he said, as he handed her the new file. He stopped talking for a moment, as if he was weighing up what had gone before. Clearly, he'd misread her reaction. 'We're very fortunate to have you here at this time. I have no doubt we can rely on your loyalty?'

She knew McCabe was now living in Washington. Avoiding him hadn't been difficult. She suspected that she'd have to face him one day but not this way. She looked straight into Krupin's eyes. For most people that would tell her something; a window into the soul, if she remembered her Shakespeare correctly. But she could shine a laser into this man's eyes and he wouldn't even blink. In plain and simple language, she didn't trust the son-of-a-bitch. She doubted there were many, if any, who did.

'Read it,' he said still looking at her. 'We'll talk some more.' He stood up.

She took the cue from him, slid the folder under an arm and walked to the door. She felt his eyes boring into her as she closed it behind her with some relief.

Back in her office she threw the file on her desk and let out a long frustrated sigh. For the past year or so, she'd lived a charmed life with few challenges, certainly none that put her under any personal stress or her in danger Writing reports and giving her government advice on sensitive political matters was enough to keep her, literally, out of the firing line. It didn't provide her with any opportunity for advancement or secure her any political scalps but that's the way she liked it. For once she was actually doing the job of a cultural and trade attaché. But the conversation she'd just had with Krupin was a clear sign that those charmed days were over. She walked to her desk, sank into the leather chair, reached out to the right-hand drawer, slid it open then rummaged inside to locate what she hadn't used or needed for several years. The thought made her sit up erect in the chair, not frightened, but tenser than she'd felt for a long time. A few seconds later, her fingers encircled the unmistakable outline of an automatic.

CHAPTER 4

McCabe was at the bottom of the driveway where he'd stood many times before. The house, a hundred yards at the top of the gravelled pathway, was the Gallagher's family home on the southside of Glasgow. Several generations of the Gallagher clan had occupied this grand old house. It was reputedly built more than two hundred years before by a prosperous local shipping merchant whose money had come from a host of dubious enterprises, including the colonial slave trade where tobacco and sugar had been the principal cargos. Whether there was any truth in this provenance, no one rightly knew.

McCabe expected his friend to be able to spin a colourful yarn. After all, that was his stock in trade. Whatever the truth, the tales seem to be embellished a little more with each telling. It fitted Gallagher's image of himself and, for that matter, those held by most people who knew him; the descendant of an adventurer, an unconventional personality, bordering on the cavalier.

Whatever its real history, later in its years, the house boasted a prouder profile when Andy's parents took up residence. They were very accomplished musicians and encouraged their family to play too, whatever their instrument of choice. Some played several.

McCabe could bear witness to that period and he had many happy memories of some summer visits. He never hesitated to accept an invitation. The quartet evenings were among the highlights which took place on Fridays in its large hallway. The surrounding chairs and the stairs were packed with admiring and grateful neighbours. Everyone in the family, that was Andy and his sister, took part. The performances continued to be staged into the winter but not with the same frequency. McCabe well remembered the ones he attended and could recall Andy playing his favourite cello. It was a lifetime ago. He doubted if that hallway had heard those melodies in a long time.

McCabe smiled as he rang the bell. Its sound hadn't changed either and it carried him back decades. He heard shoes make their distinct clip-clopping sound, hitting the stone–tiled floor, as their wearer answered the ring.

A young woman stood by the open door and stared at him for a moment without saying a word.

He began to introduce himself but she got there ahead of him. 'Mike?' she said, opening the door wide. 'Mike McCabe! I've been expecting you.'

'Irene?' he asked cautiously.

Irene Campbell with her light strawberry-blonde curls looked every bit the highland lass, with a subtle sprinkling of Scandinavian ancestry manifested quite clearly in the faint blonde streaks in her hair. While only medium build, she would catch the eye in any crowd. She nodded in agreement and pointed her well-manicured hands towards the hallway. 'You'll find it's still in there,' she said with a smile. 'Watch your footing,' she added, pointing to the large doorstep.

He remembered that too.

As she stood aside he saw the hallway behind her, just as he remembered. 'The Quartet Evenings,' he said. 'Do you remember?'

'Apparently, they're everybody's lasting memory,' she said as she walked ahead. 'I was too young to remember much. When Andy's parents passed away much of the drive for them went with them. My parents went to America and Andy lived in London.'

'How are they?'

'Fine but they don't travel much, otherwise they would be here.'

They walked through the hallway into the lounge. It looked much the same. The decor had altered and the furniture had been updated, but there was still the old dark green Chesterfield sofa that dominated the room. He remembered sleeping on it many a time, after a night out.

'I missed you at the funeral yesterday but I thought I might see you at the reception,' she said.

'I had a few things to take care of,' he lied.

She didn't seem to be particularly bothered. 'I didn't hang about for long myself. But I got your message. You're welcome to go through Andy's papers. He wouldn't mind, I'm sure. He was so proud of you. Famous international journalist and you'd started with him. He talked about you often.'

McCabe smiled awkwardly. 'I'm still trying to get my head round what happened.'

'So, am I,' she said.

'The police don't seem to be saying much.'

'Is there anything to say?'

'Well, it was all very sudden,' insisted McCabe. 'It was all very strange too.'

'I know. But there's nothing to suggest it was other than an accident,' she said looking at him strangely. 'Is there?'

'No,' said McCabe immediately, not wishing to cause her any concern. 'It's just that I don't know the details,' he added quickly. 'It's not clear to me what happened.' He didn't tell her of O'Neill's misgivings. That would certainly have rocked the boat.

'I know Mike. You're just like Andy. You have to know.'

He smiled but didn't respond to the comment. 'I gather he'd just come back from the US?'

'Yes.'

'That's where I live now,' he said, hoping he could lighten the conversation.

'Where?'

'Washington, DC'

'In the White House?' she said with a chuckle, amused by her remark.

He laughed with her. 'It is a little more modest dwelling than that; actually I live on a houseboat but it is fairly luxurious by some standards.'

'I would have expected nothing less, for our Mike McCabe.' She giggled again.

He didn't mind being the butt of her jokes. 'I guess I deserved that. I didn't mean it to sound so pretentious.'

'Mike!' she seemed to fake her surprise. 'You have a sensitive side. My word, you are a big boy now. You have matured. But I think the word is pompous.'

He shook his head slightly. He wasn't going to win this one. He returned to their earlier topic. 'Do you know why he was in America?'

'No,' she said with a slight sigh. 'He would never confide that to me. You know what he was like. I'm told you're just as bad. He'd tell me nothing. But he was chasing a story, that much I know.'

'How?'

'He was like a child with a new box of tricks when he was into something. You know what he was like. He didn't need to tell me anything. I knew him of old. That's what fired him. When he was animated, excited, you knew there was a story he was chasing. That was what drove him. That was his life.'

'Are we journalists that simple to read?' The question sounded sincere.

She didn't answer but walked to a drinks cabinet on the right side of the bookcase. She looked at the clock on the wall and smiled. 'I guess it's not too early for you Mike,' she said as she lifted a bottle and began to pour into a small glass. 'My uncle always had a stock of Black Label in the house.'

It was just after twelve, according to the clock which had just begun to chime.

'It is lunchtime, after all,' he replied with a grin and reached out towards the glass. 'So I don't mind if I do.'

'To answer your question, some are easier to read than others,'
she replied with a broad grin, as she handed him the glass.

He took a sip and scanned the room which appeared to be
acting as an office too. Books were piled up on racks of shelving
everywhere and the desk was covered in piles of papers and
folders. 'Would you mind if I had a rummage through his stuff?'

'Are you looking for anything in particular? You're just like
him; the story is everything.'

Most people would have thought the room was in chaos but
McCabe would bet there was a system in this disorder. There
was no surprise there; old habits. Andy had a curious way of
filing. The difficulty was finding the key.

'I have a few things to do, if you want to try your luck. I'll be
gone for about an hour or two.'

McCabe settled down to wade through the chaos. If there was
anything important, it was likely to be on or in, the desk
somewhere. A couple of hours later and he hadn't made any
significant progress. There was an entry in a diary; the name of a
professor with a US telephone number. A quick phone call
determined it was Georgetown University, one of the prestigious
American universities, based in Washington, only a few miles
from where he lived.

Tucked inside the diary, and clipped together, were several
sheets of paper, containing data with rows and columns of what
looked like quantities and dates, all marked *Confidential*. That
label had been used to describe everything from medical reports

to free offers from the local television company. Did they have any currency?

They could mean something. They could mean nothing. The numbers made little sense to him. That was the nature of the beast called journalism; follow a lead to its end. Invariably, some would lead to nowhere. It was a tedious process of elimination. Somewhere along the line, you hoped to get lucky.

A phone number and a list of meaningless dates weren't much to show for his efforts. He was dozing off. The tedium and the whisky, he'd helped himself to, were having their effect.

'Any luck,' asked Irene Campbell, standing by the door.

He shook his head to push away the drowsiness. 'Only these sheets and an entry in his diary,' he said pushing the book and the papers across the desk towards her. 'Do they mean anything to you?'

She read the listings. 'The figures on the sheets mean nothing to me.'

'What about the name in the diary? Does it mean anything to you?' he said, pointing to the entry.

She lifted the book and read the name aloud. 'Melvin Draper, Professor of Physics.' She laughed. 'I didn't know my uncle rubbed shoulders with such company. He didn't have an academic qualification to his name.'

'But he could spot a story disguised in ten tons of bullshit,' commented McCabe.

They both laughed.

'You found nothing more?'

'No. Can I take these,' asked McCabe, pushing the diary and the sheets into a pile on the desk. 'The sheets are marked *Confidential* but you probably get three offers a week from the local supermarket labelled the same way. I'll take them anyway, if that's OK?'

'Of course,' she said, as she walked to the fireplace. She reached up, lifted a photo from the mantelpiece, walked back and laid it on the desk. 'I found it in the desk earlier.'

McCabe studied the print. 'Who is it?'

'No idea; perhaps Draper,' she said. 'Check him out on the university site.'

'I can tell you have your uncle's instincts.'

'Not me. I teach philosophy. My approach to life wouldn't make me a good journalist.'

McCabe wasn't going down that road. He had a feeling he wasn't going to win this argument either. 'Have you a current photo of Andy?'

She went back to the mantelpiece and took out the contents of a small frame. 'It was taken a few years ago. But it's a good likeness.'

He smiled and slipped it into the pile.

'But I'll tell you one thing that doesn't need the instinct of a prize-winning journalist, 'she added.

He was waiting for the punchline, another gibe at his expense.

She walked across to the window, drew the curtain back slightly with one hand and beckoned him with the other. 'Those guys have been following me all day,' she said, nodding towards a black BMW parked in the street outside.

McCabe glanced through the space in the curtains to have a look.

She let the curtain drop closed. 'They came to the house, flashed some badges, said they were from the police and asked if they could come in to ask me a few questions,' she said, now sounding a little concerned.

'What did you say to them?'

'They claimed to be investigating my uncle's death,' she added, sounding as if she didn't believe them. 'They flashed some badges. ''So what?'' I asked them. My teenage nephew can make them on photoshop. He does IDs for the other kids in his school. The answer is no.'

He could easily visualize her looking unimpressed at their credentials and closing the door in their surprised faces. He couldn't resist laughing out loud. 'They are the same guys that were at Andy's funeral, I'm sure.' McCabe now sounded concerned. 'What do you think they wanted?'

'How would I know? I told you, I didn't let them in. They're after something. That much is obvious; clearly something my uncle had that they wanted. I don't know what I should do about them.'

McCabe glanced through the curtains again. It was definitely the same BMW that was at the cemetery and the two, seated in the car, were the duo at the funeral. He fingered O'Neill's card in his pocket. 'I think I know a guy who just might.'

CHAPTER 5

The driver's door of the black BMW flew open and one huge hand of detective, Wullie O'Neill, grabbed the driver by the collar, dragged him from the car and in one swift move threw him six feet into the road. The driver barely understood what was happening before he was then sprawled across the car's bonnet. His passenger sat frozen and open-mouthed.

Thirty minutes later the BMW duo was in separate cells in the central police station in Glasgow.

O'Neill threw a file on his desk, turned the pages quickly, picked up his phone and shouted a few instructions. Two young junior detectives were beside his desk in seconds. 'That was a pretty pathetic show. If it hadn't been for a call from a journalist we wouldn't have known where the hell they were. Fortunately, I was here when the call came in. In the end, I had to go and do the job myself.'

They both shifted nervously in front of O'Neill who turned over the sheets in the file in front of him, almost with contempt. 'Let me get this straight. God knows, I'd hate to do either of you an injustice. You follow them to their hotel, as instructed, presumably having the escape routes covered?' O'Neill stopped for a moment and looked at them blankly.

The young policemen looked at each other.

'But you didn't,' said O'Neill quickly. 'They spotted you immediately and then fucked off out of it,' he said with a long sigh.

 'Sorry boss, we don't know what happened. They got wind of us and scarpered,' said the youngest of the pair.

'A twelve year-old kid could probably have spotted you clod-footing your way all over the hotel. Your job was to subtly keep an eye on them.'

O'Neill thought for a moment, stood up from his desk and walked to the window. 'Leave them to me. But before I interview them I want to get everything we have on them. Put the feelers out. We now know when they arrived; British Airways from London three days ago; hired a car and went to a funeral. Apart from one having a crap at Glasgow Airport on his way out, which was a delicate detail I see you insisted on putting in your report, we know bugger all. Find out! I also want to know where they took Andy Gallagher's car. Got it?'

 O'Neill took a breather in the noisy crowded street outside, slowly rolled a cigarette and inhaled it deeply. There was something disturbing about this case. Despite all his bravado he knew he couldn't keep the BMW guys locked up for long. In a matter of hours, the proverbial roof would fall in and his boss would read to him his version of the riot act. He knew that but there was something in this case which smelled to the high heavens, as his mother would have said. He was willing to admit that his pride, some would call it vanity, was a little bruised. Who were these guys who just barged their way into this case?

They were claiming some national security authority. But this was his patch and Andy Gallagher was worthy of better than a footnote in some sealed file. The old boy deserved better than that and if O'Neill had any say in the matter, he'd make sure he got it. He finished his roll-up and dialled into his mobile phone. 'Put the guy who was driving the car into the interview room. I'll be there in a minute.'

O'Neill slowly climbed the stairs, poured himself a cup of water from the dispenser by the exit, crumpled the carton when he'd finished and threw it the rubbish bin. He walked quickly towards the interview room, took the files handed to him by one of his assistants and then threw the door open.

John Minter said the label on the top file. He'd been the driver of the BMW who had already sampled O'Neill's hospitality. The folder contained one sheet. It said the prisoner had been arrogant and uncooperative. He was seated at a table at the far end of the room. The bruises on his face were clearly visible, although he didn't seem concerned.

O'Neill had met his type before. Since he'd been a young constable on the Clyde, he'd witnessed them by the dozen. Some were hard but damn few. The detective entered the room slowly and deliberately shut the door with a bang. It was meant to be disturbing. The prisoner jumped at the sudden noise.

'So, you fancy yourself as a bit of a toughie, eh?' fired O'Neill without any preliminaries. 'I wouldn't go round Glasgow boasting about that, if I were you. You might find your self-esteem will take a bit of a battering, not to mention the rest of you. The folks in this part of the world are not too accomplished in the art of diplomacy, so I'd be careful if I were you.' He sat down in the chair opposite. 'We're not short of your type around here but usually we don't have much problem dealing with them,' he said as he leaned across the table then suddenly banged it with his huge right fist.

Minter jumped back in surprise.

'I really don't care a shit what you've been doing here,' said O'Neill. He stopped speaking then stared at his prisoner. It was meant to intimidate. It did. 'You see, this is my patch.' He banged his fist again on the table. 'My patch,' he repeated very slowly. He leaned as far forward as he could, almost nose to nose with Minter who looked very uncomfortable. 'My patch,' he said again, emphasising every word. 'Do you get that?'

Minter shifted in his chair and tried to look away but O'Neill had him in his stare. There was nowhere to go. 'You can't keep us here. You've seen our credentials.'

O'Neill laughed loudly. 'Is that supposed to scare me? You see, I don't care a rat's ass for your fancy credentials from south of the border. They don't matter jack shit up here. You're now on your own pal,' commented the detective with as much menace as he could contrive. 'Your boss might pull a few strings and get you out of here but I can make it pretty uncomfortable for you while you're here. And I will. Get it?'

Minter stared back at him. If it hadn't been clear to him before, it was now. It was evident that in his manor, the policeman made his own rules. Here, this rogue cop was top of the food chain.

'MI5 or whatever it was,' said the policeman, devoid of any obvious deference. 'You don't come waltzing in here without me knowing what you're up to.' He was still staring at his prisoner who looked even more uncomfortable. 'Why were you at Gallagher's funeral? What's he to you?'

Minter didn't respond.

O'Neill sat back in his chair and spread his huge hands flat on the table. 'Here's another thing for you to consider. If you don't come up with some answers, you'll rot in this gaol, as long as I can keep you here. Is that too clichéd for you or would you like a more literal meaning?'

Minter looked puzzled.

'Simply put, you're not getting out of the rat hole I'll put you in, until I get some answers. Is that straight enough for you to understand?'

Minter nodded, although he looked in a daze.

'And of course, I'll extend the same courtesy to your pal,' said O'Neill. 'That's grand, I'm glad. We wouldn't want any misunderstanding now, would we?' he added, forcing a smile. 'Let's start again.'

It didn't take long to find Gallagher's car; where else but their own police forensic unit though still under restricted access.

'The car is restricted but they didn't say anything about any report,' said the head of Glasgow Police Forensic, a long-time friend of O'Neill, sliding a folder across his desk towards the detective with a mischievous wink. 'But you're going to be disappointed. There's nothing to go on.'

'What do you mean nothing?'

'Wullie, there's not much in that statement to misunderstand. I found nothing unusual. No tampering. It is an old car with obvious defects but no tampering.'

O'Neill looked disappointed. He seemed angry. 'Shit!'

'If you're so bloody clever, what did you get out of your questioning?'

O'Neill didn't say anything for a moment. He sounded pissed off. 'I got nothing out of them and probably won't. I interviewed them separately but nothing! They were scared alright and would have coughed had they known anything. I'm convinced of that but they know nothing. They're lackeys. That's the way these guys operate. They're only told what they need to know. For operational use only; isn't that the phrase? In this case, none of the two guys we picked up has got brains big enough to hold too much information anyway. But I'm confident I've put the crap up them and hopefully their bosses too. When I put them on a plane in a day or two, we might have a few answers. Somehow, I doubt it. Have you any ideas?'

The Head Of Forensic shrugged his shoulders. 'No scientific facts to support any theory. But as far as the car is concerned there's no mystery. I wasn't supposed to examine the car but I did. As I said, there is nothing wrong with it; nothing was tampered with. I'd say Andy Gallagher lost control of his car,

42

for some inexplicable reason. I know, as a cop and his friend,
you might find that difficult to accept but it's true.'

'So why were they so concerned about keeping it a secret?'

The forensic shrugged again. 'That's an entirely different
question. I don't think they're interested in the car but what
might have been in it. I think they're looking for something.'

'That Andy had, or they thought he had?' queried O'Neill.

'Exactly and I think they still do, which was why they were
parked outside his house when you picked them up. They were
going to try his house, if they could. But you and your diligent
police work, not to mention your zealous physical welcome, put
a stop to that,' added the forensic, laughing at his comment.

O'Neill ignored the remark. 'Any idea what that might be?'

The forensic shook his head. 'Not in the slightest.'

O'Neill grinned. 'But you're right. They are still after
something. They were outside Gallagher's house for some
reason. Whatever it was they hoped to find, I'd guess, they
haven't got it yet!'

O'Neill needed another respite outside in the fresh air but
tainted with his favourite weed; tobacco. He rolled a particularly
large one and savoured the first inhalation as if it was nectar. It
was. He was hoping McCabe was made of the same mettle as his
friend Andy and, not being as constrained as the police, would
have more chance of uncovering the truth. He didn't know the
guy but he knew his reputation as tenacious and dogged.

McCabe wasn't a certainty but he was a good bet. He would share what he had with him. He pulled out his mobile.

Mike McCabe heard his mobile buzz as he walked along the gangway to the BA Shuttle flight to London. He checked the text message. It amazed him how the big policeman's hands could be delicate enough to text a message of any length.
The inspector was succinct and to the point.

Thanks for the alert. Nothing from the examination of Andy's car. The BMW morons are definitely security, looking for something they didn't find. I'm sure of that. I'll be forced to release them. Good luck. O'Neill.

McCabe boarded and did his best to get comfortable. He dialled a number in London. 'I'm on my way to Heathrow. But I have an urgent job. How are you fixed?' He nodded at the reply. 'Great! I'll send the details. I'll need it by tomorrow. See you then.'

He sent a thank-you text to O'Neill. Perhaps, with a little good fortune, the London contact he'd just dialled would discover another piece of the picture.

.'

CHAPTER 6

McCabe could hear the din before he opened the door. *THE VAT* was a typical wine bar in the city of London, the heart of the capital's financial nerve centre, frequented by the brokers, bankers, the new wiz-kids and a few of the old hands. This was where contacts were made, others renewed and rumours started or squashed. Lunchtime, like today, or early in the evening, the mix and the activity was the same.

Why he had agreed to meet in this place, a living cacophony, a veritable vibrating ear-sore, was anyone's guess. It was hardly conducive to a quiet chat. Dozens bundled their way round the bar, while others huddled into the smallest of available spaces. Stan Walker was seated at the far end of the bar guarding an empty stool. With luck they might have some comfort and a chance to talk without the need to scream.

McCabe pushed his way through the throng, slid onto the vacant seat, ordered a Black Label for himself and a beer for Walker. He took a quick gulp of his drink which arrived promptly. 'I'm sure we could have picked a place a little noisier, like a football stadium,' he griped. 'Or even a train station in the middle of rush hour?'

'OK. I get the message.' snapped Walker. 'McCabe you're never frigging happy are you? The great investigative reporter; everything has to be on a plate. For your information I was seeing someone two streets away and it's as good a place as any to meet. At lunchtime, anywhere in the City of London that is half decent is crowded, don't you know that? This is where the wealth of the nation is made, where subtle hints and deals take root. You should know that. Half of your profession does its work the same way, I'm told.'

McCabe smiled. He wasn't rising to the bait. 'Sorry, just a little pissed off. I've got to go and see my lauded editor after our session; restricts me a bit with the old booze. I thought I could avoid him but he knows I'm in the country.'

'Why restrict yourself. Tell him how you really feel. How could he possibly resist the opportunity to meet up with his favourite prize-winning reporter?' said Walker, barely disguising a smirk.

McCabe and Walker had history. There didn't seem to be a time when they didn't know each other. They'd met up when they both were cub reporters working on rival local newspapers. Walker's weekly paper folded and he ended up on the local radio station which worked well, for a time, until he was discovered screwing his boss's wife. Walker accused his boss of being petty-minded. So did the wife. Nevertheless, Walker was fired and the wife divorced.

It also forced Walker into a change of career path. Now his research skills, second to none, were sold to the highest bidders. Whatever the secret, he'd find it. It was a remarkable talent. There were few places to which he couldn't gain access, to the surprise of a whole range of miscreants, from thieves to adulterers. Walker was good at what he did and he loved it.

Despite the banter, McCabe trusted him implicitly and the information he uncovered.

The truth was that Stan liked adventure, risk and all the things he'd read about in boys' annuals when he was a kid. Some of the pedestrian and routine tasks of daily journalism bored him. When he went to a local council meeting, he wanted to discover a story about corruption and bribery. Invariably he would end up writing a story about a change in the parking permits. In his new role, he was like a dog with a bone.

He did have one weakness. His appetite for sexual adventure was measured in risk and danger. No matter how attractive the woman, it was his preference that she be married and their illicit rendezvous take place in the family home, shortly before hubby returned from his labours. The tighter the deadline, the happier he would be. These were sexual dalliances accompanied by the thrill of the chase.

McCabe took another swig at the scotch. 'I'm not in the mood for any wind up, Stan. Tell me what you've got.' He sounded tetchy.

Walker took a hefty swallow from his new beer. 'It was quite difficult getting some of this stuff. As luck would have it, I knew the very guy tuned into this sort of thing.'

'What sort of thing is that then?'

Walker had another drink from his beer and ignored the question. 'McCabe, you know damn well what we're talking about here; government.'

'Perhaps I shouldn't ask how you got the information then?'

'What do you care?'

'Well, how did you get the information?'

Walker touched the end of his nose with the index finger of his right hand. 'What you don't know won't harm you. You should have more sense than to ask me such a question.'

'Should I?' laughed McCabe.

'Have I ever let you down?' said Walker, winking in return. 'He's a retired government security guy, if it makes you feel any better?'

'What does that mean? You don't need to answer. I can guess. He was caught drinking on the job and got ousted.'

Walker distorted his face a little. 'He got caught alright but screwing his manager's wife; stupid ass.'

'I thought you had that franchise?' replied McCabe unable to resist the comment.

'I'll have you know, I've never been as careless as this dumbo. I've only once been caught on the job by a husband,' said Walker, sounding very serious. Clearly, it was a matter of pride.

'I thought that was part of the thrill,' chuckled McCabe as he waved to the barman and ordered another round. 'I mean the danger, all that sort of stuff.'

'I'm not as ham-fisted as this guy; total amateur, out of his depth. Anyway, she was a real slapper. I wouldn't have considered her a challenge; no contest, no points!'

McCabe poured the newly arrived drink into his old glass. 'I think that is as far as I want to go with this. I take it that despite his stupidity in the sexual stakes, he's a reliable source? If this guy is a has-been, he's not going to be much help to me, is he?'

Walker pushed his empty beer glasses towards the barman and sampled the new one. 'You should be more open-minded McCabe. This guy still has good contacts, well sometimes.'

McCabe looked impatient. 'Why are you so obtuse? Is he reliable or not?'

Walker smiled. 'You're a student of humanity, Mike, are you not?'

McCabe waited for the punchline.

'This guy is a social chameleon,' said Walker slowly.

'Which means what exactly?' asked McCabe still sounding impatient.

'Because of the contacts he gets invited to all sorts of events and because he's yesterday's man he can sit in any company and nobody pays the slightest attention to him. Socially, he's a nobody. He blends into the background giving the impression he's not interested; perfect.'

'In what?'

'In whatever the gossip is that's being traded. He absorbs everything and has a bloody good memory.'

'OK, I'm convinced, he's a good source. But is he the right one and plugged into what I'm after?'

'In that business you never know. You get scraps then try and put them together. The bits are likely to be totally unrelated.'

'I know that. You didn't have much to go on but the question is simple enough. What was British Intelligence doing at Andy Gallagher's funeral? '

Walker pulled out a small notebook from inside his jacket.

'There are a few strands that I've been trying to put together into some recognisable pattern.'

'Well?'

'There are a lot of people in British Intelligence concerned about one issue at the moment.'

McCabe moved forward in his chair. 'Which is?'

'It concerns the nuclear facility in Georgia, ex-Soviet that is. A consignment of nuclear fuel was removed, at the end of the trouble there, supposedly by the US for safekeeping.'

McCabe shook his head. 'That's not new. The story was in every news outlet. The Americans flew it to Dounreay. I know that much. That wouldn't interest Andy Gallagher. He was a committed newsman. And the spooks, I told you about, who were at his funeral, must have been after something else.'

Walker looked a little puzzled. 'Well, that's the problem.'

'I don't follow you,' said McCabe, finishing his scotch and nodding to Walker to reorder.

'The stuff didn't arrive.'

McCabe shook his head. 'It did. According to all the press reports, it did.'

Walker signalled to the barman and reordered as instructed.

'The US delivered a consignment alright but it wasn't the one from Georgia.'

'How do you know that?' asked McCabe, watching the barman pour the beer.

'More correctly, it couldn't have been the one from Georgia,' added Walker.

'Why?'

Walker sampled the newly arrived beer. 'I like this,' he said, looking at the glass. 'It's going down a treat.'

'Back to the story, please,' insisted McCabe.

Walker continued drinking as he spoke. 'They had a spillage in Dounreay, shortly after it was delivered. Perhaps that was what interested your friend?'

'I can't see why that would be of interest to him unless it was really serious and it led to something else. They have those pretty frequently.'

Walker played with his glass for a moment, moving it a few inches across the bar and back again. 'It wasn't serious.' He stopped and drank some beer.

'Well, what's the story?' asked McCabe, now sounding frustrated.

'My source tells me that they did the usual checks and they found nothing,' blurted Walker followed by his cheeky grin.

'You mean a small leak that didn't mean anything. No contamination?'

'No. I mean, they found nothing'. Walker stopped and stared at McCabe. 'It was harmless.'

'That's what I said,' shouted McCabe, trying to make sure he was heard above the increasing bar noise.

'Mike, you're a man of words. Listen to me carefully. Their tests proved that what the Americans brought to Dounreay wasn't radioactive.'

'What the hell does that mean?'

'Mike, who is being obtuse now? It means that whatever they delivered to the north of Scotland was not what they took from Georgia. Perhaps that is what your friend Gallagher had discovered and the spooks wanted to know about too?'

'So, what was it? And give me a straight answer this time.' McCabe had run out of patience.

'My source didn't know.' Walker hesitated for a moment. 'What he did know was that the consignment was no more dangerous than a bloody wrist watch from the nineteen fifties.'

'So what's going on? Where's the real stuff?' pushed McCabe. He was sounding irritated. Walker took another swift drink from his glass and settled onto his chair again. He nodded, as if he'd just had a brainwave. He looked a little smug. 'What they brought from Georgia wasn't radioactive.'

McCabe looked a little impatient. 'We bloody-well know that much.'

'Hear me out,' defended Walker. 'You can really be impatient, sometimes, if not most of the time.'

'OK,' conceded McCabe. 'Let's have your brilliant deductions.'

'Simple logic; let's work it out. And don't be so supercilious. You really can be an asshole.'

'OK, OK. I'm sorry. Let's have it.'

Walker smiled. 'First option, they made a mistake and picked up the wrong thing? Unlikely! Second option, they lost it on the way; also unlikely. The last option, they swapped it en route; possible but can't say why?'

McCabe thought for a moment. Walker's logic was sound, he supposed, but it didn't take them anywhere. 'What did your source say?'

Walker hesitated then shook his head. 'He really didn't know. There are all sorts of rumours around, he claims. But they're only guesses.'

'Rumours, like what,' pressed McCabe.

Walker shook his head again. 'I thought you wanted facts? You're always lecturing me about facts.'

'Tell me,' said McCabe, firmly.

'Where would you like me to start? That the Americans had a buyer for the stuff; that they would plant it and use it as an excuse to invade some unsuspecting trouble spot, or the most popular, that the CIA wanted to use it as bait.'

'What? You can't be serious?'

'You can't catch a lion with a tin of dog food, Mike.'

McCabe smiled. 'Very profound, Stan, but that's a dangerous game. One wrong move....'

Walker interrupted. 'It's only a rumour. Maybe the Russians have heard it, that's why they're so nervous?' He laughed out loud.

McCabe didn't respond to the joke. He didn't find it funny.

'Who would blame them? 'So what did the Americans take out of Georgia?'

Walker shrugged, finished his drink then looked at his watch 'Sorry, Mike, that's all I've got. I must go.' He stood up to leave. 'Would any of this have interested your pal Andy Gallagher?'

McCabe nodded. 'You can bet your life on that.'

'

Hanya Smolka arrived at her apartment in Bethesda. NW Washington. She loved it, so Americana, light years away from the grey concrete monoliths of her Moscow residence which had no architectural merit and even less aesthetic value. For years, in Russia, those drab surroundings had been her home. The lives of those she'd left behind hadn't improved as hers had done. The faces of the neighbours, fond though she was of them, reflected a miserable drudgery and daily struggle that was indelibly etched even in their smiles. She was as powerless to assist them as they were to help themselves. Not surprisingly, there were few photographic mementoes hanging on her US apartment walls.

She stopped as the door closed behind her and listened carefully. The small clock on the wall in the hallway made its usual subtle ticking; everything else was silent. She walked into the lounge and quickly inspected the room; nothing had obviously been disturbed. It was her standard routine. But today she sensed an intrusion.

Not for the first time had she imagined someone had been in the apartment. Usually, they were not clumsy, the clues never blatant; just the hallmarks of professionals. The realisation that she'd had a visitor was as disturbing as the invasion itself. What she'd sensed was subtle but after her inspection she was sure. A vase slightly out of position, a drawer not fully closed and a rug a little offline. She was a professional too with an eye for detail who'd been trained to notice. Someone had definitely been in the apartment.

After her conversation with Krupin, it had crossed her mind that he would run his own checks on her, inspect her home and invade her privacy in search of something incriminating. Or at least something he could use to support such a claim. She'd like to think her thoughts were ludicrous. But she couldn't get them out of her mind. The business she was in nurtured such underhand behaviour as much as it did fear and suspicion. The latter was corrosive and destructive, and it was easy to let the imagination take hold.

Perhaps Krupin wasn't looking for anything but was planting something instead, an incriminating item he'd find in a later inspection? She didn't trust Krupin. That was a recipe for all sorts of mayhem and she couldn't allow such thinking to take root.

She dropped her bag on the sofa, her shoes on the carpet and her tired self in the armchair by the window. The conversation with Krupin kept replaying itself in her head in one endless monotonous and tedious loop. The tone of the meeting was easy to determine but its purpose less so, and his motive she could only but guess. She had only known him a matter of months but there had always been some form of tension between them; two people who were supposedly playing on the same team but she was never sure if their goals were the same or indeed the rules that they followed.

Her lifestyle was considered too risky by some, by others it was bordering on treason. She knew her own people had searched her apartment several times. She'd found a few listening bugs in the obvious places. There would be others. They were definitely Russian made. They weren't the only intruders. The Americans had visited too, of that she was certain. However, that was the price for her lifestyle and she was prepared to pay. For her, an apartment in the secure and claustrophobic confines of the Russian Embassy was no alternative. But these signals told her she needed to be careful.

As she pulled the cord to close the curtains, she suspected that the surveillance team from the adjacent building monitoring her apartment would change tack now from video to the audio with the emphasis on the concealed listening devices in the apartment and the listening bugs on her telephone. They were the Americans.

She poured herself a generous glass of vodka, only slightly doused with a tonic water and a handful of ice, then settled into her chair by the desk, near the window. The first mouthful barely touched the sides. She felt it hit her stomach and then her brain as she sank back into the chair. She felt much better.

With her free left hand, she flipped through the pages of Krupin's file. She was probably breaching another code by bringing it home.

At first sight, there didn't appear too much to get upset about. A consignment of nuclear fuel had been taken from Georgia a week before by the Americans for safekeeping, at least that was the inference or more accurately, it was the assumption. A British installation in the north of Scotland was considered the favoured destination. The US had more than hinted at the plan weeks before. The Russians has given it unofficial approval. But now, for some unexplained reason, the US would confirm nothing.

Hanya Smolka had another mouthful of the vodka. She stared at the pages from the file, now spread across her desk. There were photographs attached to the folder, one of a journalist called Andy Gallagher, whom she'd never heard of, who apparently had tutored the young Mike McCabe. She smiled at McCabe's photo, a characteristic pose of him sitting on a bar stool with a drink in his hand. She'd guess it was Black Label scotch and probably a generous measure too. The snap was five years old.

Her memories of him were much older but just as fresh as if they were from yesterday. She'd often wondered after their meeting in Moscow, if she'd ever see him again. Those days seemed a million years away from where she was now. So was he. The junior reporter she had met, who had fumbled his way through elementary Russian, delivered with his characteristic confidence, was now an international journalist, rubbing shoulders with global power brokers but apparently without compromising too much on the journey.

The McCabe she had known then could barely contain his ambitions. He was looking for a story behind every face; a story within a story. In fact, that was one of the games they used to play. They would study a person, chosen at random. One of them would make up a story involving the character, at least in part, and the other would finish. It was good fun. They never knew if they ever got close to being accurate. She laughed at the memory. Certainly, it was fun.

She turned on her laptop, inserted a few choice words and studied the outcome on the screen. She took another mouthful of her vodka and leaned back in the chair again. The cuttings, which poured onto the screen, told their own story. In Europe, Asia and America, Mike McCabe had made his presence felt, usually wading through some political quagmire on the wrong side of the power balance. She read the cuttings, some written by him, some by others about him. He had as many critics as he had admirers but she guessed he didn't care. He'd always thought the powerbrokers were fair game as was any detour they made from the straight and narrow. He'd been kicked out of several Third World quasi-republics with amazing regularity. That was no great feat. Journalists of lesser standing had managed that with not much effort, but getting kicked out of the US – or at least been threatened – was quite an accomplishment. Few managed that in the Land of the Free Press and the US Constitution. In reality, McCabe's London editor had recalled a outraged reporter, as a political compromise, before the threatening mud hit the fan.

She flipped through the file again. It didn't say why McCabe was involved in this incident which so worried the Russians.

Knowing him, he didn't know either but he had an instinct that lured him to the core of any story.

She'd met him in Moscow in the most extraordinary of circumstances. He was a young reporter representing a British wire service in a press party of travel writers who were covering the inaugural trip of a major UK bus company attempting to copy the American 'Greyhound' model. The idea was that American backpackers would arrive in London on some cheap airline flight then buy their bus ticket to Russia. The coach, as it did in the press trip, would wind its way through Warsaw, Minsk then on to Moscow through the bleakest of countryside. The route, cleared by the authorities, was not meant to be scenic. It was a road that would keep them well away from anything that may have had any military significance.

That's when they met.

She was then newly graduated from the then Moscow State University, an extraordinary linguist who spoke perfect English and whose party credentials made her the favoured and trusted comrade to fraternise with the western press. She was full of confidence, she recalled. She'd been told that her selection was because of her charm and charisma which was matched only by her intellect, a sharp and clever mind that was capable of dealing with the chaotic frenzy surrounding a greedy and arrogant corrupt western Press. She'd been embarrassed by the accolade then and felt even more so now.

She liked McCabe from their first meeting. They found themselves isolated from the pack one night, more by good fortune than by any clever planning or design. Fortune seemed to follow them that evening. While the rest of the group chose, erroneously it turned out, to recover in their hotel after a tiring day of predictable and tedious staged propaganda with no real insight into Russian life, McCabe had requested a tour of Moscow.

Whether it was her stunning looks and McCabe's faltering Russian which had attracted the locals, she would never know. But their reward was a table in a small family-run restaurant off Red Square with questionable service and a meal that was barely mediocre. But it was real Russia and an experience neither of them would ever forget. Another dimension soon surfaced. Whether it was his pathetic Russian again that was to blame, they never discovered, but they were thought to be a newly-wed couple, who in traditional style found themselves the toast of every table in the restaurant in what appeared to be some spontaneous nuptial salute. He didn't know until later what had happened. She had known, having easily spotted his earlier grammatical fumbling. But she'd said nothing and made no attempt to correct him. She was glad she hadn't.

However, she was later to find out that their supposed intimate dinner was not so. They'd never been alone. Their every move and sound was recorded. She had never said anything about that either.

What was she to do; just walk into McCabe's life, as if nothing had happened in the decades that had passed. It didn't take much to work out their logic. The journalist's reputation dictated that he would rock the boat and the truth would emerge. If she stayed close to him, she'd share in any exposure. It sounded all too simple and while McCabe might be a cavalier, he was no fool and with little effort would know their motive. Perhaps he didn't mind being a stalking horse. It certainly would be fun being together again. She hoped he'd feel the same.

 The third and last photo in the Krupin file was of a Georgetown Professor of Physics, Melvin Draper. It didn't tell her much except that he'd been a presidential adviser on nuclear fuel and was chair of a Senate Committee on national security issues. The rest she would have to discover for herself.

Andrei Krupin, obviously anxious, watched the arrival of a black Mercedes below his window in the driveway of the embassy. He could see quite clearly a tall thin man in the back of the chauffeur driven car. The driver raced to the back, opened the door and saluted.

 Krupin shivered slightly when he caught a glimpse of the skeletal features of Colonel Nikita Solokov whose reputation was as frightening as his appearance. Well known as an enforcer, he looked the part, as he glanced about him and up towards the window.

Krupin darted back behind the curtain to prevent being seen. He shivered again at the possibilities that could lie ahead. It was no coincidence that the enforcer had arrived at this time. There was no reason for such a visit, he'd assured his superiors in Moscow. He'd sent a letter by secure diplomatic courier and attempted to follow it up with a phone call. But no one seemed to be available to take his call. He sensed then that he hadn't been believed and that he might not get the opportunity to plead his case.

It wasn't the first time he'd witnessed such decisions made in absentia. The condemned, in anxious silence, waited for the outcome and even longer for it to be conveyed. His first inkling came in the form of a tip-off from an old friend.

Too many were not pleased with the information he'd sent through, his source warned. There were no details, no obvious strategy and no real intent to solve the problem, they'd decided. Essentially, they believed, he was not taking the issue as seriously as he should, that he needed some help and they'd discussed a number of options. He was a little short of friends among those at the meeting and there were few prepared to argue his case. There were even fewer who would put their own reputation on the line and their heads above the shaky political parapet. Such strategies were rarely advised and only on occasions when there was obvious gain.

Apparently, a significant number of the group had been for his immediate removal and to be ordered home to an uncertain and undisclosed future. In the end the consensus was in his favour. He would survive the day, but only just and at a price. Given the other options, he should be grateful, claimed his source. It could have been much worse. There were some who would have had him eliminated.

Krupin lit another Sobranie, despite having one burning in the ashtray on his desk. He knew his progress, or lack of it, would have found its way to the top in Moscow and now had filtered its way down, acquiring a more hands-on approach. A consignment of atomic fuel housed in a research institute in Mtskheta, near the Georgian capital, Tbilisi, had been taken by the Americans to prevent it falling into the hands of terrorists or a hostile nation. The Russians had sanctioned the move. But now they were convinced that the Americans had done something else. The most disturbing rumour was that the fuel was being used as bait. The determination of the US security agencies, to take extreme counter-terrorism measures, had made this reckless plan believable. The Americans had denied the stories but had done nothing to disprove the assertions. Every day without clarification fed the rumour and with it Russian fears.

The information was in Washington, he was told. The measures taken so far had proved ineffective. They needed to be, in American parlance, pro-active. Solokov was the solution. He was here to give a helping hand, so the missive dictated. It had come in code over the embassy's secure email network, although he trusted nobody and suspected the Americans knew about it before he did.

How the enforcer would implement his strategy, Krupin could well imagine. The Russian hadn't acquired his reputation by being subtle, just effective. Now he was bringing his particularly crude style of persuasion to Washington.

It had taken Krupin some time to adapt to the way the Americans conducted themselves. Curiously, their security agencies were accountable and while they bent the rules to obtain some ends, those who did knew the risks; they would be on their own and outside the law. He tried to explain that climate to Moscow and how things were much different in the US than back home. He knew he walked a fine line with such explanations; the subtle border between information and criticism. Of course he wasn't suggesting that everything he'd been taught was a lie but there were marked differences between the theory and the practice. He needed to be very careful in his comments and not leave himself open to being branded *Pro-American*. He knew such labels could have fatal consequences. The problems Smolka had in the wake of such accusations were proof. Had she not been well-connected, who knows what would have been the outcome? He was not so fortunate. Clearly, the arrival of his visitor from Moscow left little doubt that his arguments had failed.

There were other dangers too, inherent in Solokov's crude approach and his reckless strategies. He'd lived and worked in an environment where he enjoyed total freedom. The methods he employed were of his own design and his behaviour was an example of the crass and the primitive. Krupin had told Moscow bluntly that such methods were inappropriate in Washington; apparently, without success.

 He and Solokov shared the same rank, at least in theory. But the visitor's experience in frontline combat was an enviable addition to his impressive intelligence portfolio, which Krupin could not match. Consequently, the enforcer's contacts, particularly in the military, were formidable and the strings they could pull would have significant influence.

Not surprisingly, Solokov didn't expect any opposition or obstacles to his game plan.

Krupin looked frightened. He inhaled deeply the last remnants of his Sobranie cigarette then stubbed the remainder in the ashtray on his desk. He opened the window slightly and tried to waft some of the smoke and odour from the room.

He was determined to hold his ground and to await results.

Solokov, he suspected, wasn't.

Neither was Moscow.

CHAPTER 8

McCabe had been walking in the rain for nearly fifteen minutes and had now abandoned the idea of a cab. He should have remembered that in London when it rains, predictably, the taxis disappear. It was a cultural mystery he had yet to solve. 'Bugger, it!' he murmured. 'I'll walk.' He was glad of the chance to put his thoughts in some sort of order. So far he'd found that difficult. Maybe a walk in typical London drizzle might do the trick? It would be therapeutic, one way or another.

He buttoned up his coat, walked away from the main road and took the pathway along the river. The boats which frequently ferried passengers up and down the Thames, were ghosts of a bygone age when the most efficient transit had been by river. Now they were almost commonplace, carrying tourists and workers on regular scheduled trips.

He felt the rain hit his face as he sat on a bench by the riverside. Heavy drops hit the river surface, creating small ripples in the water. As the downpour got worse, the circles disappeared and the river now splashed about erratically. He was cold but found it refreshing. Perhaps it would clear his head and act as a mild antidote to his lunchtime indulgence.

So, what was the story so far and what did he have? Precious little! The information he had didn't amount to much, nor was he able to link any of the bits together. There was little point gathering scraps of data without seeing how they related to each other. When in doubt go back to the beginning. That was the basic rule.

He tried but the list made it no clearer. He had a friend, a mentor, who'd died in a car crash with no suggestion of foul play; he'd met a local detective who was adamant that everything was not as it seemed; he'd acquired a photograph which may or may not have any relevance; he'd collated a bundle of papers with meaningless data; he'd discovered from Gallagher's personal files an American phone number and address in Washington. They were strands which yielded no recognisable pattern. Perhaps they never would?

His instincts told him otherwise. He agreed with O'Neill, the tough Glaswegian cop. Not all was what it seemed. While the cause of the death was not suspicious, the timing triggered a number of questions. They centred around Andy Gallagher's activities before he died and the interest they had generated among some third parties. Those were enough indicators to tell him he was on the right track.

Half an hour later, totally drenched, McCabe finally arrived at the office for a meeting with Edmunds, the head honcho of his newspaper. On some occasions, those encounters had been tedious and trying, this time it would be mercifully and unexpectedly short.

Scott Edmunds was a talented and clever man, an obvious product of expensive private schooling followed by a predictable spell at Oxford University, studying the usual Philosophy, Politics and Economics (PPE), the standard educational program for those destined for high office. He excelled in neither educational institution but was well-suited for the seat he now occupied.

McCabe had mixed feelings about him. He respected Edmunds' intellect and envied his contacts book, which had the personal phone numbers of every cabinet minister who'd served in government over the previous twenty years. But he couldn't trust him.

Their relationship had never been close. It had never truly survived an episode a few years earlier when, without any discussion, Edmunds had appeared to buckle under pressure from some power brokers on Capitol Hill, unhappy with the waves created by a very tenacious McCabe. The editor had acquiesced and withdrawn his troublesome correspondent. Edmunds' version was that a high-flying politico had given him warning that any future visa, granted to a working journalist from the *London Daily Herald,* was in jeopardy unless McCabe was recalled.

McCabe was disgusted. He considered it an affront to journalism and the repugnant episode was a crude method of silencing him and gagging what was supposed to be a free press. In the end, he was never sure what the truth was but he hated being recalled, particularly under those circumstances, and deeply resented Edmunds for doing so. In his eyes, there was little to separate Edmunds from the politicians under whose pressure he had folded. McCabe came from a background and a world well removed from the political cosmos in which

Edmunds found comfort. In time, the broken fences had been mended, although patched would have been a better description. The good news was that Edmunds was on his way out to lunch and would be gone for the rest of the day. The bad news was that he still had time to deliver his dictates.

'Come with me to the car,' he ordered. 'I was sorry to hear about Gallagher,' he added softly. 'I know you were fond of him.'

McCabe said nothing but walked beside Edmunds, as commanded. He looked uncomfortable.

'Gallagher had made a few waves in the weeks before his death, I gather,' said Edmunds. 'Is that something you're also working on?'

McCabe, emotionless, stared straight ahead. He had to tread carefully and not get dragged into something, of which he didn't know the consequences.

He'd learned not to concede too much ground when having discussions with Edmunds. . Once the door was slightly ajar he would establish a foothold and before long McCabe would find himself on the back foot. He was determined not to commit himself to anything.

'I hear there are several other parties interested too,' Edmunds said, obviously fishing. That was his style. 'National security, I'm told,' he added without any qualification.

McCabe stayed silent.

He could picture the group huddled together in one of their clubs drinking brandy after a good dinner, exchanging idle political gossip, which had emanated carelessly from the mouth of some inebriated cabinet minister. Whatever the circumstances, Edmunds was firing a warning shot or perhaps he was just showing his vanity. It wasn't wise to ignore the advice but he found it difficult to just tug his forelock and accept the intelligence blindly. It wasn't in his nature.

'Told by whom?' McCabe asked quickly, sounding cynical. He should really have kept his mouth shut but he couldn't. He was irritated by Edmunds' mind games and his patronising rhetoric. The editor was no fool but to dismiss such insight would be stupid.

Edmunds sensed the reluctance. Characteristically, he just smiled. It was his version of 'piss off', which he was much too polite to say. However, it meant the same thing.

McCabe knew the code and smiled in return.

Edmunds got the message.

The editor slipped into the back seat of the car and slammed the door shut.

McCabe watched the Jaguar turn at the traffic lights about a hundred yards down the road. He felt like following it with a two-fingered gesture. But, of course, he was much too polite to do so. He laughed out loud.

Had time allowed, it would have been nice to revisit his houseboat in Chelsea Harbour, currently rented out to a young high-tech entrepreneur on the road to making his first billion. Soon the wiz-kid would be able afford a fleet of houseboats all his own.

In Washington he'd leased something similar from a friend. It wasn't the same. But it was a fair substitute.

After a relaxed night in London, he boarded an early British Airways flight from Heathrow to Dulles, more than a little relieved that this emotional journey had come to an end.

Seated at a desk in a small room at the back of the third floor in CIA Headquarters, Langley, Virginia, Aiden Johns was starting his day. There was nothing to suggest it would be any different to the dozens that had gone before in a career which was comfortable but had stalled.

As a researcher, it was his job to trawl through magazines, newspapers, published academic papers and a host of databases in the public domain, looking for intelligence which the Agency might find useful. In cooperation with colleagues, dedicated to the same discipline, banks of data were assembled so the operators in the field, whatever their assignment, would be well briefed.

Economies, traditions, festivals, holidays, preferences, religions, sports and dozens of other characteristics that painted the pictures of diverse global cultures were investigated, listed and categorised. He and the others who performed the research would plough through everything they could read which had been published, extract the information they thought useful, then enter it into the relevant section in their database. From academic papers to political speeches; they were all read, analysed and assessed.

Rarely did he have any direct contact with the operators in the field but he hoped his efforts proved useful. He would get the occasional phone call or email asking for more information. Those contacts would be few and praise unlikely. He never found out the purpose of any supplementary enquiry. But, at least, they gave him some encouragement and indicated that someone read his work. Sometime in any year, he would be rewarded for his diligence in the form of a salary review, perhaps a rise. That was his lot.

Also as part of the routine, he'd scan a number of databases, largely designed to monitor the movement of people coming into the USA. Whatever their profile or rank, any person entering the country had to do so via its ports, borders or airports.

With the aid of a clever piece of software developed by a colleague, he would interrogate a listing compiled by Immigration and the FBI. Originally meant to alert the authorities to anyone entering the US on suspicion of counter-intelligence, it was now a valuable tool in the fight against terrorism.

Particular nationalities were highlighted as were any points of entry near military or utility installations; Chinese, Russians, Iranians and a list of nations considered to carry potential threats. Major conurbations were also deemed a target, particularly the seat of power in Washington.

The clever software detailed the description of the individuals accompanied by photos, their place of entry, the declared purpose of the visit and their supposed expertise.

73

He entered the usual commands into his computer and inspected the results. There were the usual and predictable mixture of business people, engineers, academics and tourists. Entering the west coast there appeared to be an unusually large influx of religious groups, representatives of churches and movements of which he was unfamiliar. He shrugged and smiled to himself. . Unofficially, he gave particular attention to those travelling on diplomatic passports. It was a sector considered open and vulnerable, where diplomatic license could be abused at the risk to national security.

The tedious daily task was almost over when an entry made him lean forward and peer at the screen. It was the profile of a Russian who'd just arrived at Dulles Airport, Washington. An alert accompanied the entry.

Johns immediately switched to another classified database. There the Russian was listed in comprehensive detail.

Colonel Nikita Solokov, retired Russian army, ex-KGB, security expert and agent. Now, he was flying a diplomatic flag, joining the Russian Embassy in DC as part of their trade delegation. He had been suspected of carrying out a number of assassinations in as many countries.

Johns doubted the Russian's unique talents could be harnessed to advance international trade. An immediate alert of his presence in the US would be fired up the chain. Perhaps today would prove to be surprisingly interesting after all.

CHAPTER 9

After more than eight boring hours of air travel, McCabe touched down at Dulles International in Washington, DC. He was subjected to the usual grilling by Immigration then gratefully collected his luggage from the carousel before jumping into a cab on the steamy sidewalk outside the terminal.
 He was tired as he dropped his bags in the lounge of his houseboat. It was almost six in the evening and he needed a drink. He poured himself a cold beer from the fridge and a large Black Label from the cabinet. His routine on arrival from the UK never varied; stay up as long as he could to get into local time. He'd usually manage about nine o'clock, then exhausted from his journey and assisted by the warmth of a few whiskies and a meal, he'd slide into bed. It went to plan this time too and by nine-thirty he was fast asleep.
 The rocking of the boat woke him early. He could hear the trucks delivering the fresh fish to the market at the far end of the quay. It was just after six. He felt refreshed. Within five minutes he was on deck watching the commuter traffic make its way through the park opposite. He loved living on the water. It was different and made him feel he was removed from the pack. He rented this one, although he owned something similar moored in London's Chelsea; an old coal barge that now had all the trappings of the English middle class, a far cry from its earlier life. This one, part of a floating community in a marina on the

Potomac River in Washington, was now home. It was the same for dozens of his neighbours who enjoyed the idyllic waterside haven.

 Ten minutes later he was showered and on his way to a local restaurant for breakfast. Smoked haddock with poached egg, toast, orange juice and coffee would kick-start his day. As he looked across the estuary, it seemed such a long way from Scotland, and what he was doing now was so different from the life he had shared with Andy Gallagher, so many years ago. Thoughts of the previous days came back in waves, as did the tiny fragments of what he'd discovered. In truth, he hadn't discovered anything of importance, nothing that gave any shape. Andy's niece had been helpful, had let him take the few documents they'd uncovered which might be significant; O'Neill had added his few pennies worth to the confusing picture; and Walker had given his touch too.

 Andy was pursuing a story. There seemed little doubt. However, whether any of these elements, including the interest of the two MI5 bozos, was connected was anyone's guess. A check on the Georgetown University website confirmed the identity of the American professor in Andy's photo. But what was the link? Perhaps he was just a friend, a drinking companion, a dinner guest? Maybe there was nothing sinister at all. The Glaswegian detective had been adamant there had been no evidence of foul play in the crash but he was equally confident there was something amiss. His instincts told him so.

McCabe's concerns echoed those sentiments, He finished his breakfast and ordered more coffee with a little Black Label to give it a kick. He would let Washington waken up then he'd take a trip to Georgetown and visit the professor. Perhaps he might then get some insight?

He was experienced enough to know that most investigative or detective work was pedestrian, even dreary. Hopefully, somewhere along the road a pattern would emerge. Frustratingly, a few unconnected roads might need to be travelled before the right one, but as he kept reminding himself, such was the nature of the beast.

McCabe sauntered back to the houseboat. The quayside had come to life now with the activities of the fishing boats replaced by the river cruisers, preparing to carry the hundreds of tourist up and down the Potomac.

He made his first batch of coffee of the day, filled a mug then added another small capful of Black Label to it, just to fortify himself before he went on deck. The residential part of the marina was filling up quickly now, as boats returned to their berths from their winter trips to sunnier climes.

'Can I have a word, Mr. McCabe,' came a shout from behind. McCabe turned to spot the manager of the marina, several hundred yards away, walking with one of his determined strides. He was on a mission and heading McCabe's way. In less than a minute he was walking up the gangway.

The manager was a nice old gent who always dressed in a navy blue blazer jacket and a nautical-styled cap. McCabe doubted whether he'd ever had any connection with the sea but he was very personable and everyone seemed to love him, despite his obvious eccentricity. His visits were usually provoked by a complaint from a neighbour, most of the time trivial. The residents called him 'the Commodore' which appeared to be more a nickname than a title. He loved it nevertheless and answered to it with pride.

'Can I have a word, Mr. McCabe?' he repeated.

'Do have a cup of coffee, Commodore; just made,' replied McCabe.

'No thanks'. He seemed a little on edge, if not embarrassed.

'This is a little awkward,' he said quietly.

'Do sit down,' said McCabe, directing him to a chair opposite his. He leaned forward. 'What can I do for you?'

'As I said, it is a little awkward,' he repeated.

McCabe was a little surprised. It didn't sound as if he was about to discuss something trivial. He looked quite earnest.

'You know strictly speaking we don't allow subletting here'. He was obviously uncomfortable and fidgeted a little in his seat. 'I like to be flexible, as you know. I've never made an issue of you using your friend's boat. We are very happy to have you here, Mr. McCabe. But the others, your friends, have made life a little difficult.'

McCabe looked puzzled. He had no idea what he was talking about. He was about to challenge him but the Commodore continued without a breath. 'I saw them myself, about an hour ago, and thought they were visitors, so I didn't bother. Your

78

neighbour in the next boat thought you were still away and challenged them. He reported it to me. They claimed they were friends and you'd given them permission to use the boat.'

McCabe said nothing for a moment. He raced downstairs to the lounge, across the room to his desk and pulled at the drawer. It gave way easily, slid out at the lightest touch as did the splinters where the frame had been forced. The drawer was empty. He couldn't remember what had been in there.

The Commodore stood by the door.

Had he been able to see McCabe's face, the look would have said it all. But the journalist's back was turned and his voice disclosed nothing.

'I take it they weren't your friends?' asked the Commodore with an official voice. 'I need to file a report in case there is an insurance claim. Is there anything missing?'

McCabe was trying to get his thoughts in order. His reply was barely audible. 'No, nothing,' he murmured. 'It was probably someone from my office; a misunderstanding. No need for anyone to be worried. I'll check it out and let you know.'

The Commodore seemed a little uneasy. 'I still have to file a report,' he insisted.

McCabe was now back on deck and gently easing him from the door towards the gangway. 'It's nothing Commodore. I'll talk to the neighbour who alerted you. He can be a bit imaginative sometimes. There is no report needed. I'm sure there is a simple explanation.'

McCabe successfully ushered the Commodore down the gangway then raced back to check the cupboard at the back of the lounge. It had been disturbed alright, but the papers he'd brought from Scotland, so carefully collated by Irene Campbell, were still intact.

He had a quick inspection of the rest of the cabin. Whoever came aboard didn't appear to have disturbed anything else. If they had succeeded, what would they have got anyway; a couple of sheets of paper with a few notes scribbled by Andy Gallagher, a photo and telephone number of a Georgetown professor? Big deal!

What had they been after? Perhaps they didn't know themselves? Maybe they just wanted to find out if he knew anything at all. He couldn't discount the possibility that the break-in was not connected to Gallagher or his data. His instincts told him otherwise. The houseboats were subject to the same security issues of any urban dwelling, opportunist thieves and professional burglaries. If, as he suspected, they'd just targeted his modest houseboat, neither of those explanations made any sense.

McCabe switched on his laptop and keyed in a few instructions. A photo of the professor and a brief bio appeared on the Georgetown University website. There was no doubt it was the same man. McCabe read the impressive accolade; Professor of Physics, adviser to Congress and to two Presidents. There were several other photos on the academic's page; several of him in the White House with the US Presidents and their staff. The photos were all group shots, except one; a one-on-one with the chairman of the Homeland Security Committee, Senator Dorman Forsyth.

Certainly, the professor was a player alright but what was the game?

Returning from a modest lunch on the lawn outside his office, Aiden Johns got back to his chores. The list of periodicals and academic papers he'd read in the latter part of the morning had made him drowsy. The academic world had once been his goal but poor pay and the thought of teaching undergraduates were two good reasons to seek pastures elsewhere. The agency, so far, had proved to be a fairly acceptable alternative. But sometimes the work could be tedious. Then something would catch his eye and lighten up his day.

He read and reread an article sent from a contact in the UK. It was from a local newspaper on the north coast of Scotland. The sender thought the coverage unusual. After several reads he agreed. He signed onto the publication's website and read even more. It was amazing coverage and given the subject matter, it did seem strange.

The newspaper reported that the Americans had delivered a consignment of nuclear fuel from Soviet Georgia to Dounreay. The newspaper's editorial ranted about a new cold war where terrorism and nuclear weaponry combined to produce an uncertain cocktail of instability. While it was always good political strategy, it claimed, to have a bogey man: one that could distract the populace from real issues, the fears were real enough now, with attacks in France, England, America and Spain. These were testaments to the new order.

The news coverage definitely seemed strange, Johns thought, given the frequency that such types of deliveries were made to the Dounreay complex. The people who worked in the Scottish installation, and those that lived in the vicinity, were used to nuclear fuel arriving at the facility, some for processing, some for storage and containment. An American cargo plane had been used for the transport; nothing unusual. He looked puzzled. He studied the reports again. There was something wrong. He couldn't put his finger on it but there was something that didn't make sense. The provocative editorial and accompanying headlines were meant to draw attention to the story. Why?

To add another dimension, the newspaper claimed that the British government had announced it would transport the fuel by ship from the Scottish complex to the US Government's nuclear facility in South Carolina,

'Why not take an advert out on national television,' whispered Johns to himself. He typed a few instructions into his computer. There were plenty versions of the story online. Most of them said the same thing.

It has been announced by the British Government that 5 kilograms of enriched uranium, originally taken by the United States from the Soviet Republic of Georgia to prevent it falling

into the wrong hands, will be taken to the US in the interests of national security.

He typed in a few more commands then moved nearer the machine to read the text carefully. It was an extract from an academic paper. It was a little verbose, typically obscure pretentious prose, but the message delivered to a recent conference in Washington, DC was clear to those who had the background, the education and the intellect to follow the reasoning.

What interested him wasn't what it said, but more what it implied. Unless he was wrong, it may have put into context what he'd just read in the Scottish articles.

The author of the paper was one of his ex-professors; *Melvin Draper, Professor of Physics, Georgetown University.*

CHAPTER 10

Professor Mervin Draper stared out of the window across the forecourt of Georgetown University. He watched the students pour into the campus, over the manicured lawn, past the statue of the university's founder, which loomed over the entrance, as they made their way to a mid-morning lecture in the halls of the main clocktower building. He could hear the noisy waves of chatter and footsteps as they climbed the stairwell, passing his office door en route to the main hall at the end of the corridor. He smiled at the bubbling enthusiasm. Wish that they were talking about his subject.

He turned back and looked towards the old fashioned telephone answering machine at the far end of his office. He knew it was a joke among students who considered it a technological fossil. Few could resist making some remark when they visited his office and saw it for the first time. In a curious sort of way, he liked their response. It added to his reputation as an eccentric. At least, that's what he hoped.

Usually, when he'd been away for several days, the messages piled up. Not so now. The only message it contained was a surprise, as was the identity of the caller.

'Professor, this is Andy Gallagher phoning from Washington, Dulles Airport on my way back to the UK. I'm flying overnight and will be back home early morning local British time. I think you were right about what we discussed. I have some numbers that seem to support what we chatted about over dinner on the last night of the conference. Sorry I've missed you. I'll try and contact you again when I get back to Scotland. Cheers.'

Draper sat at his desk, opened the right hand drawer, pulled out a small cardboard file and opened it. He studied the contents, as he turned the pages very slowly. The theory they'd talked about, after way too many brandies, was plausible but only just. They didn't have enough information, he'd said. He'd remained unconvinced at the time and had laughed at the journalist's conclusions but now he wasn't so certain. There were certain incidents that couldn't be explained. As a scientist, he'd always built any hypothesis on a bedrock of fact and, as was the procedure in any credible research, others should be able to look at the same data and arrive at similar conclusions. Such was the essence of what was called 'peer review'. Simply put, any other researcher with access to the same information could emulate his experiments and support his conclusions.

But the hypothesis, which had emerged from his discussions with Gallagher, was bordering on the preposterous. He was a journalist and was allowed that latitude when writing a story. Conjecture, he would call it. In the scientific world, it was erroneously speculative with no proper data to support it. Such a research paper could not be 'peer reviewed', so in academic terms it was worthless.

He couldn't worry about that now. He had a lecture to deliver.

McCabe found the lecture hall without much difficulty and sneaked into the back row. He tried to follow the content of the lesson but was lost after the first sentence. Particle physics was not his strong point. He could join the trillions of others whose education was equally limited.

Draper was totally immersed in his subject. It was unbridled rhetoric. The professor seemed oblivious to anything around him and certainly to what his students were doing. He was immersed in his own world, some several light years away. A few students appeared to take notes on their laptops and tablets, some looked as if they were asleep, a couple played games while the rest were busy answering their emails.

At the end of the lecture, without a word or gesture, Draper packed up his chattels and made for the door. The students, familiar with the silent cue, did likewise and with little noise gathered up their books, closed down their electronics and made for the exit too.

McCabe was caught unaware and was well behind the professor as he raced to his office. Two flights of stairs and a little breathless, he was in front of the closed door of Draper's office.

He was about to knock when it was opened suddenly by a student on the way out. 'The professor is busy today,' she said. 'Too busy to see anyone,' she added a little caustically.

McCabe looked past the student to the professor on the telephone.

He waved and beckoned McCabe to come in.

McCabe stood awkwardly in the doorway while Draper finished his call. The book-lined office was far from plush. The furniture looked well-worn and the style dated, not that there were too many surfaces visible. Not surprisingly, it was a sea of papers, stacked from floor to ceiling, also on every bit of available desk space. Of course, how could it be any other way?

Draper finished his call and pointed to the seat in front of the desk.

McCabe inspected the chair piled high with papers.

Draper moved quickly, lifted the bundle and dumped it on the floor. 'End of term papers; must be finished by the end of the week. There is an endless line of students pressurising me. They all want to know how they've done.'

McCabe smiled, trying to look sympathetic.

'Thanks for the call earlier. I didn't know. Sorry to hear about his death. How did he die?'

McCabe wasn't sure about the answer to that question, neither was the Glasgow police. But he tried.

'It was a motor accident.'

'How did it happen?' asked Draper predictably.

'We don't know.'

'We?' asked Draper.

McCabe was feeling uncomfortable, trying to put together an explanation that made any sense. He wanted to be asking the professor questions, not the other way round. 'There's nothing suspicious,' lied McCabe. 'But the police are checking some details.'

'What would they be, Mr.McCabe?' There was no easy way to change direction here. He'd underestimated the professor. He should not have been surprised; this man was a top mind. It was stupid to even try. He stopped scrambling for an explanation about Gallagher's death. 'I don't know any more, neither do the police, although they assure me that no one tampered with the car.'

Draper nodded and ceased the questioning.

McCabe doubted he was satisfied with the explanation. It was unlikely; no one else was.

'Yes, he was very popular with the students.'

'Students?'

'Yes, he did a couple of guest lecturing stints for me. It was the only time they ever stopped answering their emails or playing games.' He laughed, as he said it. 'Don't look so surprised, Mr. McCabe. I do know I don't command their attention, all of the time.' He laughed again. 'But Andy did. He had a way with them. He related. It's a gift.'

'What did he lecture on?'

'He talked about research, how to go about it, how to manage it. It's a dry subject – Research Methods we call it – but he made it interesting. They loved his talks; full attendance too.'

McCabe appreciated the background note and he could understand why the students loved the lectures. But he needed to press on. 'Why I'm here is that I believe he was working on a story. I don't think it caused his death but I think it's related.'

Draper shook his head. 'I'm afraid I can't help you there. I didn't really know him.'

'You said he did some guest lecturing for you,' challenged McCabe. He was unhappy with the answer.

'Mr. McCabe we have many guest lecturers here. I sometimes don't even meet them,' said Draper, looking momentarily at the answer-machine.

The glance hadn't escaped McCabe. He pulled out his notebook, flipped through a page or two, read down a list of items then closed it. This seemed to unnerve the academic. 'According to his diary, you and he were to have dinner together at a conference which you both attended about a week ago.'

Draper looked uncomfortable. 'Those dinners are attended by dozens, if not hundreds. I was the after-dinner speaker at one of those sessions. That's what he probably meant.'

McCabe wasn't buying the explanation. He could sense the professor's discomfort. What was he afraid of that would make him lie? 'Let me get this straight professor. The conference at the *Mayflower Hotel*, was attended by hundreds, as was the dinner at which you were the principal speaker?'

The professor nodded. 'Yes.'

'And you don't recollect having dinner with him specifically?'

'You don't at conferences,' said Draper, sounding a little offhand.

McCabe wasn't happy with the explanation and he was far from finished. He pulled out his notebook again. The professor was getting visibly more uncomfortable. 'Two men from British

Intelligence appeared at his funeral and at his house the following day. I believe they were looking for something. Can you imagine why?'

The professor was taken aback at the mention of the intelligence duo. 'Two men from British intelligence,' he repeated.

McCabe said nothing for a moment and let the silence have an effect on the professor's obvious nervousness. 'Yes. I won't go into the details but they searched his crashed car and later were caught by the police stalking his house, with the intention, they believe, to ransack it.' That wasn't the entire truth but McCabe thought the drama might have some effect. 'Have you any idea what they would be looking for?' he added.

Draper stood up. 'I don't think I can help you any further, really, Mr. McCabe.'

McCabe felt he had him on the run and he had a few things he wanted to say before this show was over. He rifled through the notebook again, just to increase the theatre. The more nervous the professor got, the better might be the result. 'According to his mobile phone records or cell phone, as you call it, he telephoned you, several times.'

Draper instinctively looked at the recorder.

McCabe caught the glance again. 'I'll bet that if you played back that machine,' he said pointing to the unit, 'I'd hear a message from Andy Gallagher.'

Draper began to move towards the door. 'I don't wish to be rude, Mr.McCabe, but I cannot help you anymore,' he said slowly, emphasising the words.

McCabe walked with him. But he hadn't finished yet. His punchline had yet to be delivered. 'Two men broke into my home, here in Washington, yesterday. I think they were after some documents I had brought back with me from Andy Gallagher's house in Scotland. What do you think they would be looking for?'

Draper didn't utter another word as he ushered McCabe out of the office.

CHAPTER 11

The Mayflower is one of the classiest hotels in Washington with a fairly impressive heritage. During the Second World War, its restaurant was reputed to be a hotbed of espionage. Supposedly, diplomats, politicians and seedy traders of misinformation frequented its tables at lunchtime and dinner trading their wares. Spies of both sexes plied their favours in exchange for information; so the legends claim. How many of the stories are true is left to the imagination. Certainly, in those days, it acquired a reputation, beyond its culinary excellence. Today, the hotel is happy to promote the myths to the hundreds of tourists who now enjoy the establishment's hospitality.

McCabe laughed quietly to himself at the bar overlooking the restaurant. In some respects not too much had changed, he thought, although the political game that was now played within these walls was more subtle in nature. Consistent with the profile of the world's capital, there was no shortage of lobbyists or apologists selling their version of the truth to politicians whatever their divide. Also, there was no lack of politicos willing to believe them. Such was the machinery of American government and those who greased its wheels. On some occasions, it was not only the mechanism that got greased.

McCabe had some personal memories of the hotel. On earlier visits to Washington, before the prevalence of cell phones, he had used the hotel's spacious phone booths as a makeshift office. They were equipped with a comfortable stool, a door for privacy and, leaning on a small shelf below the telephone, he was able to compose and file his stories to London in relative comfort. It was a bygone age. After the hotel's recent refurbishment, it was now likely to be a computerised business hub.

But he wasn't sending word to London today. The hotel had been the venue for the conference, attended by Draper and Gallagher. According to the professor, there had been no private dinner but they would have dined with dozens of others, discussing a range of topics dealing with energy. The reasoning seemed vague and it didn't explain the prominence given to the entry in Gallagher's diary.

McCabe had looked through the schedule for the conference which hadn't been removed from the web. From the blurb, the conference appeared to be a typical scholastic jamboree with the competing intellects and egos jousting and preening themselves. Nothing too violent ever emerged from these forums except perhaps a bruised ego, wounded pride or a cry of plagiarism.

'It's all part of the game, another entry on their CV,' said the hotel events' organiser who slipped onto the barstool beside McCabe. Everything about the twenty-something young man appeared well-ironed; jacket, shirt, trousers and even his hair.

'Thanks for giving me your time,' said McCabe. 'Would you like a drink?'

93

'Yes I would but I'm afraid I can't. I'm still on shift. I got a brief telephone message from my boss about you but he didn't tell me your interest.'

'I'm doing a feature on conferences,' McCabe lied, sounding convincing. 'So I was using the Energy Conference, staged here a week or so ago, as an example. Would that be OK?'

'Sure!'

'I managed to pick up the schedule,' said McCabe placing a copy on the bar.

The manager inspected the printout. 'Yes, some people present papers, others are just here for the ride. As I said, it looks good on their CVs. I'm also surprised why some bother.'

'What do you mean?'

The manager looked about him, as if to ensure he wasn't being overheard. 'It's not unusual for them to be delivering papers to less than six people and some of them would be asleep.'

McCabe chuckled. 'What do you mean?'

'If it's not a ticketed event, some in the audience just come in off the street for a free doughnut and coffee, particularly if it's raining.'

'You're joking?'

The manager had a chuckle this time. 'No. You would be surprised.'

McCabe delved into his inside pocket, in search of Gallagher's photo. 'The conference delegates have communal dinners, I understand, but is there a seating plan?'

'Sometimes but come coffeetime they move about. However, there was no seating plan in any of the dinners in that conference. A lot of people meet a lot of people, that's another reason why they're here; to see and be seen. As I said, it looks good on the CV.'

McCabe managed to locate Gallagher's picture and laid it on the bar. With it he placed Draper's photo. 'Did you ever see these guys together, at dinner or anywhere for that matter?'

The manager looked closely at the two figures, lifted the photos and studied them carefully. 'I don't recall seeing that guy at all,' he said pointing to Draper. 'Definitely not,' he added, shaking his head. 'But the other guy yes; twice I think,' he said, as he pointed to Gallagher. He peered at the photo closely. 'Yes, I'm certain.'

McCabe looked puzzled. 'Are you sure?' He wasn't expecting that answer. 'Where?' he asked quickly.

The manager looked towards the restaurant and nodded in its direction. 'Over there.'

'You saw him twice in the restaurant? During the conference?' The manager nodded several times. 'Yes.'

'But not with this man?' asked McCabe pointing to Draper.

'No, definitely not.'

'Are you sure?'

'Yes. He was with the senator.'

'Senator?' quizzed McCabe.

'Senator Dorman Forsyth.'

Hanya Smolka slid the curtains in her apartment to one side. She could see the cameras, mounted on their tripods, protruding through the window of the apartment opposite. The Americans, she'd had it confirmed, watched her day and night, her phone calls were tapped and everything she did or said was logged. She doubted it made interesting reading. She was a prime candidate for recruitment, she had been told. She still laughed at the prospect.

It was ironic because, on the other corner of the block, were the Russians. They were a little less obvious in their Ford saloon, but quite recognisable. A twelve-year old, with basic observation skills and no security training could spot them with little effort.

She was the meat in the sandwich. The Americans were watching her because she was Russian and the Russians were doing the same because she was too American. Had it not been so serious, there was something theatrical about the whole thing; a classic farce.

However, this latest problem added another dimension to the charade. Whether Krupin really needed her in this project or his devious, scheming mindset was playing games with her, she didn't know. Perhaps it was an opportunity for him to test her loyalty? She would find out soon enough. It would be fun meeting up with Mike McCabe again.

She sat back in the chair by her desk, typed a few instructions into her computer and checked the results. A clear photo of Professor Mervin Draper appeared on the screen, less flattering than the one in the Krupin file. According to her brief, he was chairman of one of the Senate's Security Committees and had been an advisor to a number of presidents. He would be the man, she'd been told, who would know what had happened in Georgia, where the consignment had been taken and for what purpose? But no one really knew. The file she'd been given was all guess work. Different theories and rumours were dotted all over it. It was the work of Russian security analysts, in an attempt to satisfy their Kremlin masters. But it had no currency. There was no concrete information. The only thing that was certain was the uncertainty. The insecurity was triggering paranoia.

Whatever she did and how she did it would be done her way. Of that she was certain.

She went into the cupboard in her bedroom and picked out a blood-red jacket with matching hat. There was nothing subtle about the outfit. It wasn't meant to be. Fully dressed in it, she looked like a beacon which could be seen for half a mile. She smiled then laughed. That was the idea.

The next bit of the plan was easy. She partially closed the curtains in the lounge but left enough room for her watchdogs to get a clear view of her sitting wearing the red outfit. She placed a matching red scarf over the back of the chair. For a while they'd see what they thought they saw, giving her sufficient time to slip out of sight. They wouldn't be caught for long but it should give her the time she needed. By then she would be gone.

Two cabs later, she walked into the campus of Georgetown University. Dressed in jeans and a baseball cap, it had been simple to slip out of her apartment unnoticed. As she walked through the main gates of the university and across the lawn in front of the clock tower above the main building she looked in every sense the all-American girl; no different from the dozens who milled around her. She stopped for a moment and glanced about her. Had she managed to slip her jailers? All appeared clear.

She climbed the steps in the main building and checked the noticeboard on the first landing.

Five more minutes and she was outside Draper's office. She had her story ready. It was perfectly sound and simple. She was a trade attaché from the Russian Embassy and had a few questions on recent movement of nuclear fuel. It was an innocent enough question and to seek his advice was legitimate enough. If there was anything to hide and the professor was a party to it, she would soon know. It was a direct approach, certainly. If there was any subterfuge, its directness should take him by surprise. She was supremely confident she could be convincing. Not for the first time had she tackled such a challenge. She turned the doorhandle slowly, it gave way and she slipped inside. The office was empty.

She hadn't noticed the figure of Aiden Johns coming through the main gate behind her. Also, had he seen her he would have recognised her; the face and profile were more than familiar. But he did neither. He was on the same mission. He walked cautiously in the corridor shadows at the time she slipped into the professor's office.

She wasn't there long before she was interrupted by what looked like a student, seeking the professor. She left in a hurry.

A wave of bodies appeared from nowhere in the corridor outside the office; an exodus from the nearby lecture hall. The figure pulled back into the shadows again and let the torrent pass. It was five minutes before he felt it safe enough to emerge. He looked around and decided to take his chance. The office door slid open easily to the touch. He closed it quietly behind and quickly scanned the room. The computer on the desk was active, the monitor scrolling screeds of data. It wasn't until he moved towards the back of the desk did he see the body. He didn't wait to examine or identify him. He was at the door in seconds, prised it open quietly, determined it was clear outside, slipped unseen into the corridor then down the stairwell of the clock tower and safely outside. Grateful and with ease, he merged with another bank of students as they made their way to the campus exit. He looked scared as he passed through the gate. Something had gone seriously wrong.

Johns raced down the side street by Georgetown University, looked over his shoulders as he pressed the remote car lock, hurriedly opened the door and sat breathless in the driver's seat. He could hear himself panting. He was sweating badly and his heart was pounding. Why did he go there in the first place? The more he thought about it, the more insane had been the idea.

His job at the Agency was primarily as a researcher. He wasn't an operator used to dealing with those awkward and physical situations. Confrontations were standard occurrences for those operatives who were trained for that purpose. Not so him. His job was to trawl through the tedious lists of research papers, published articles and speeches from obscure conferences. Most were boring and tested his devotion and professionalism in every instance. Generally they were the products of academics or similar who, in exercises of lateral thinking, liked to float their theories. Normally, he would read a paper, research the hypothesis a little further, check out any other papers or articles written by the same author then categorise it accordingly. Generally, there was never anything that required urgent action or gave him cause for concern. His job was to précis the conclusions of the author or academic, write it in simpler language then pass it up the chain for those above him to consider. He got little feedback, if any comments at all. He would nod and chat to colleagues as he came and went from his cubicle in an open-plan office but rarely did their conversation focus on work. In some projects, he had worked as part of a team, but for the most part he worked alone.

 On this occasion he had thought the idea expressed in Draper's paper was interesting. It didn't initially spell danger. But he should have recognised the signs and followed his usual procedure by passing on the details for others to consider. He'd decided to do otherwise because he'd known Draper. A talk with his old professor would be fun too.

 In retrospect, the visit was a bad idea which, initially, seemed innocent enough. He'd thought about phoning the professor or even sending an email to make an appointment. But the idea of leaving any electronic footprint unnerved him. There was no logical reason for it. He guessed it was a reaction to the world in which he lived; surveillance and phone tapping. After all, this man had been an advisor to presidents and congressmen. For some, the professor would be a natural surveillance target.

He had put his reservations aside and decided to visit the professor, like a fellow researcher, wishing to ask questions and follow-up one of Draper's research papers. As he sat in the car, the logic behind his thought process seemed warped. He'd met the professor alright but there was no dialogue; no discussion over the ideas in his paper. Draper was lying on the floor with, what appeared to be, a serious head wound. He didn't check the body nor call for help. He'd panicked. Suddenly, he'd felt vulnerable and unable to explain his presence. He ran, out of the office, down the stairs several at a time then out into the campus lawn. He could barely catch his breath. It was then that he saw him; the skeletal frame and pallid features of the Solokov. There was no doubt and it was obvious the Russian had seen him too.

CHAPTER 12

Lieutenant Pat Kovarik, Detective, DC Homicide Police, got the call when in the centre of town. He glanced in the rear-view mirror, turned the car around quickly, narrowly missing an oncoming truck then sped to the address in Georgetown. As usual, the traffic was a little congested as he left the main street and headed for the campus, with waves of students mixing with the locals and tourists looking for a place to have lunch. He pushed the siren onto the roof, let it scream for a few moments then manoeuvred the car through the meagre space reluctantly given by a line of self-absorbed drivers. He fumed, shook his head and poured a torrent of abuse towards the windscreen. Just as well, no one could hear.

Ten minutes later, he pulled the car up in front of the campus, walked quickly across the lawn beside the clock tower and climbed the stairs to an office on the second floor. He checked the note he'd made of its number and dodged yet another wave of students before he found it.

John Henry Smith, one of the police-officer assistants, was beside the door already talking to a few students. Predictably, they were female, attractive and seemed totally absorbed in what he was saying. They hadn't quite got to the swooning stage yet but that would come. John Henry, with his striking African-American good looks, had charisma. He didn't flaunt it; he didn't have to. It was effective enough without promotion. As usual, he was modest and totally focused on his work.

 He saw Kovarik, stopped talking to the students, stepped forward to meet the detective then flicked open his notebook. 'Male, mid-fifties, professor of physics; found here in his office by his secretary this morning when she arrived about nine.'
'Time of death?'

The young policeman hesitated. 'The attack, as far as we can determine, took place late afternoon, early evening yesterday. But he's not dead. He's been taken to the hospital at the far end of the university.'

'Then why am I here?' asked Kovarik bluntly.

'Judging by his wounds, he was thought to be dead. The paramedics were here in quick time and found him still alive. I haven't spoken to them yet, but it definitely does look like attempted murder.' John Henry, with the help of two patrolmen, moved the assembled students away from the entrance to the office. 'Crime Scene Police' tape now secured the corridor.

 Kovarik, still glowering, watched the students leave. 'Just what we need, the paramedics tramping all over the crime scene' muttered the detective, stopping at the entrance to the office. 'Where?' he asked and stood waiting for direction.

 The young policeman looked at him without saying anything. There was not much he could say that would satisfy Kovarik when he was in such a mood. He'd been there before and learned to ride it. It was better not to rise to the bait. He turned and pointed to some chalk markings on the floor in front of the

103

desk. 'It's not accurate but it was the best I could do under the circumstances.'

Kovarik stepped forward towards the outline, positioned about two feet from the front of the desk. He walked round it like a tiger stalking its prey. He didn't say a word but studied the marking carefully. He bent down to inspect the area closely, occasionally turning towards the desk.

The young man had seen the routine before too.

During this ritual Kovarik didn't take a note. It was meant to form a picture in his mind, to get inside the crime scene. That was his style. 'What do we know?' asked Kovarik, continuing to walk around other parts of the room.

The young policeman cribbed from his notebook again. 'A well respected member of the faculty. Tenured, full professor, all that stuff.'

'What does that mean?' he asked quickly.

'Sorry, Lieutenant. I didn't want to bore you with the obvious. He has all the academic trappings, teaches undergraduate and postgraduate students, researches and writes books and papers'.

'OK, OK,' responded Kovarik waving his right hand in the air impatiently. 'I get the picture but I want to know the things that will help us find who tried to kill him.'

John Henry didn't say anything. He knew the detective's philosophy, one he'd ingrained into his team. Two fundamentals were drilled into them; know the victim and the crime scene. Those would define the crime and be crucial in catching the killer. 'He had lectured in the morning and had office hours in early afternoon.'

Kovarik looked blankly at him.

'They're written on the door. That's when he is available to see students, out of teaching hours. '

'Do we know if any student came to see him?'

The young policeman looked awkward. He hadn't had time to investigate that element but he hated giving the detective a negative response. 'No, Lieutenant, not yet but some professors insist that the students make an appointment, apparently, he allowed them to walk in if he was free.'

'What are you saying?'

'There's probably not an appointment schedule.'

Kovarik inspected the desk, taking care not to disturb anything. It was layered with notebooks and loose-leaf papers. He lifted a few with the tip of his pen and peered underneath. 'I thought a tidy room meant a tidy mind?' he asked looking at the desk and around the room. 'So what state was his mind in?' He stopped and stared at the desk. 'How the hell could he find anything in all this?' He looked at the computer screen which had been left on. The unit displayed rows of numbers and dates. 'You're pretty computer literate. Can you make anything of this?' he said, pointing to the screen.

John Henry stepped forward and studied the figures. 'A spreadsheet of some description,' he said quietly. He could tell it wasn't the answer the detective wanted.

'I gathered that much,' said Kovarik walking to the far end of the room and inspecting the printer. He pointed to its light, felt the plastics carefully then pulled out its paper-tray. 'It's recently been used. Perhaps that's what was being printed,' he said pointing to the computer screen. 'Were there any witnesses?'

'I don't know that yet, Lieutenant'.

The detective looked thoughtful. He looked at the computer, then at the printer and back again. 'I wonder,' he said to himself.

'What's that Lieutenant?'

Kovarik didn't say a word but stood very still staring at the computer. 'The attacker might have been printing that and got disturbed,' he said pointing to the screen again. 'Then we need to get the computer checked for recent print commands.'

'I spoke to forensics but since he isn't dead I didn't push it,' said John Henry, cautiously.

Kovarik's cell phone buzzed. 'Really?' he asked. He slid the phone back into his pocket. 'No progress from your professor but he's still unconscious. We need to find out what happened. But we can't wait. You know what to do; strip search this place and check every phone record you can get your hands on. Any problems let me know.'

He walked to the window and inspected the view across the campus lawn. Predictably, students were everywhere; walking, running, sitting and some even studying. 'What do you think they are?' asked Kovarik pointing towards the gate.

John Henry stepped forward. 'At a guess, I'd say that was a CCTV system, wouldn't you?'

106

CHAPTER 13

John Henry readied himself for a tiresome and demanding the day in the professor's office in Georgetown. It was going to be as thorough a search as was possible, leaving little opportunity for Kovarik to ask him any awkward questions. He stood at the door of the academic's office and mentally compiled a checklist.

He'd had to wait to ensure forensics had finished. The department's computer experts, attached to the forensic team, had already taken the computer and would be reporting on its content soon. The other forensic specialists had inspected the crime scene and would also disclose their findings. Together, the basic scientific data would describe the crime and its consequences. Their inspection finished, it was now clear for him to move in.

The Lieutenant requested the computer experts check the recent print commands. If the data displayed on the computer had been a motive for the attack, the command would be registered on the machine and the technology experts would detect it easily enough. He also hoped they could interpret the figures on the displayed spreadsheet.

The answer-machine needed examining too and the professor's telephones, office and cell phone records, were other obvious sources. Nothing would be left to chance. Any gaps in the procedure, Kovarik would be sure to spot.

John Henry had trouble isolating the professor's office. While he had ensured the *Crime Scene Police* tape encircled the office and the surrounding parts of the corridor, it didn't stop the most inquisitive and determined students, who enquired about missed lectures and when their papers would be graded. It tested even his patience.

He quickly read the brief one-page preliminary report which had just arrived on his tablet from forensic. It needed some clarification which he would get once they had collated all their inspection data but they were able at this stage to estimate the time of the attack. It was around mid to late afternoon the day before, they claimed, which confirmed his original estimate.

He then checked the summary sent to his tablet by the computer specialists. There had been a command to print activated on the computer. But it hadn't been sent to the printer. Did that mean the assailant didn't have time, had been interrupted or there were two different people?

He checked the content of the printer; nothing but blank paper. A young girl popped her head round the door. The young policeman winced a little. 'Didn't you see the police tape outside,' he said with one of his characteristic warm smiles. He didn't really want to spend more valuable time explaining to yet another student the procedure. If it had been Kovarik she'd interrupted, the rhetoric would have been quite blunt. 'What can I do for you young lady?' he said, still being charming without displaying any hint of annoyance. 'If it's about lectures or marked papers you really need to go to the faculty office.' He forced another smile then returned to inspecting the printer.

'No, no,' she said quickly. 'I heard you had been interviewing some students to see if they saw or heard anything,' she added as she moved further into the office.

'Yes, I've been talking to some,' replied John Henry cautiously. He certainly wasn't in the business of updating a nosey student.

'I saw a person in the office.'

John Henry moved towards her. 'You saw who?' he said, now with obvious interest.

'I don't know if the person I saw had anything to do with this,' she said, not quite confident.

'What time was that?'

'Somewhere between five and six, I think,' she answered, sounding a little vague. 'I haven't worn a watch since I broke up with my boyfriend and he gave me the last one. I didn't want to buy....'

John Henry lifted his two hands. 'I get the picture,' he said forcing another smile. 'The man you saw; can you describe him?'

'No, no!' she said instantly.

'You can't describe him?' John Henry was about to say something which would have been more characteristic of Kovarik. He looked unusually impatient.

'I mean, it wasn't a man. It was a woman.'

'A woman?' he stuttered. He couldn't disguise his surprise. 'Can you describe her?'

The girl thought for a moment. 'It's not easy to do that, is it?'

John Henry sighed quietly. He knew from experience some supposed witnesses were far from reliable and, needless to say, so was their testimony. Some, who had seen the same thing, barely yards from each other, would testify the complete opposite. Some couldn't remember but, unwittingly, made up details since they thought it was expected of them. What category would this student's testimony fall into? However, he also knew every piece of information could be valuable. It was his job to decipher what was valid or not.

He nodded to himself and remembered the lessons drilled into him by Kovarik. 'Try, do try,' he said, encouragingly to the student.

She looked thoughtful.

He was hoping she wasn't about to make up what she couldn't remember.

'She was tall for a woman, I'd say, blonde and pretty.' She stopped and seemed in thought again. 'Yes, that's it; definitely pretty.'

'Anything else?'

'She had a baseball cap on, so I could only see part of her face.'

'What kind of baseball cap?'

The student looked blank.

'Did it have a colour or a logo or anything distinctive?' asked John Henry, trying to coach her towards some answer.

She shook her head. 'I really can't remember.'

'Did you speak to her?'

'No,' she said shaking her head. 'I thought she was from our computer department, fixing the professor's machine. He was always having trouble with it. I don't think he is too tech savvy.'

'Are you one of the professor's students?' John Henry asked, as he took notes.

'Yes and no!'

John Henry's look was enough for her to instantly clarify her remark.

'Sorry, that was a stupid answer. What I mean is, I don't take his lectures but I help him out occasionally with number crunching.'

'Can you be more specific?'

'It's a thing called Operational Research.'

'You'll need to explain that to me, I'm afraid,' he said, apologetically.

'It's about taking data and being able to identify a pattern from it. It's not always obvious and needs a certain amount of numerical skill and the ability to analyse or interpret the figures.'

'What kind of data?'

'I'm not actually sure. They were about the movement of nuclear fuel. I could show you but you've taken the professor's computer away.'

'I think I have the idea,' commented John Henry, still taking notes. 'Can I have your name, please?'

'Caroline Bennett; I'm third year physics,' she said, as she wrote a note on a piece of scrap paper and handed it to him. 'That's my cell phone.'

Before he could ask her anything more, she was gone. But her statement was a bonus which would add a little more colour to the report he would give to Kovarik.

An hour later, his examination of the office had produced nothing of any consequence. Now he would return to police headquarters and go through the paperwork he'd collected from the professor's desk. Whether any of it would give them a clue to the crime or its motive was anyone's guess.

With a bit of luck the telephone invoices for the office phone and the professor's cell phone might yield something.

That was part of the Kovarik drill too; check, check and check again.

CHAPTER 14

Senator Dorman Forsyth appeared a little disturbed as he parked his car, he nodded to the security man as he passed through the detector, swept through the corridors of the Senate building to his office then beckoned the young woman staffer behind the desk in the outer office to follow him. He dropped into his leather chair behind the desk. 'You took a message from a professor in Georgetown yesterday. The note you made of it where is it?'

'I left it on your desk, sir. I typed it up. It's headed *urgent*.'

The senator appeared harassed. He hurriedly raked through the different piles of paperwork on his desk, producing little but more chaos.

The staffer, without fuss, joined the search with an immediate and better result. From beneath a small stack by the edge of the desk, her hand emerged with the note. She tried not to look triumphant.

He snatched it, read it quickly then sat down. He seemed a little calmer as he murmured a reluctant thanks and waved her away. He read it again and again.

He pressed the intercom on his desk. 'Apart from what's on the note, did he say anything else?'

'No, sir; not a word,' she said. 'Not one word!' she repeated.

The senator went to a filing cabinet at the opposite end of the room from his desk, to the left of the door into the outer office.

He produced a key from his pocket, quickly checked over his shoulder that he was out of sight, flipped through the folders in the top drawer, pulled out a thin white file and placed it on top of the rack. He opened it, read the first page slowly then did the same for the remaining sheets. He returned the complete file to the cabinet, slowly walked to his desk, picked up the note about the professor's call, read it again before he curled it up into a ball inside a clenched fist.

The staffer had excelled in brevity. 'Please return the call immediately, *urgent*,' it read. There was no ambiguity; succinct to the point, although it didn't explain why the urgency and what had triggered it. However, there was one serious problem.

He spread a copy of the latest edition of the *Washington Post* on his desk. A picture of the Professor was prominently displayed on the top right-half of the newspaper. The story attached claimed he had been attacked and had been taken to intensive care in *Georgetown University Hospital*. The police had launched an enquiry. Clearly, he wouldn't be returning phone calls anytime soon.

Kovarik was pleased with John Henry's efforts and told him so. The detective liked the young policeman, his style, his dedication, his concentration and his focus in the face of plenty of attractive distractions from the opposite sex. Kovarik hadn't known there were so many attractive young women in the police headquarters. They seemed to emerge from the woodwork when John Henry was around.

In this case, he'd done an excellent job combing the professor's office for clues and embracing the task of inspecting the academic's phone records over the last year; and without complaint.

It was now a murder enquiry. The professor had succumbed to his wounds and died without gaining consciousness, so they didn't have the benefit of the victim's testimony which might have given them a head start. So, crime scene evidence was crucial.

As yet, the news was not in the public domain. Kovarik had decided to keep the death quiet as long as he could. The more the details of the crime were only known to his investigators, he felt, they had the edge. But he knew he couldn't contain it for long. After every interview the task of keeping a lid on the news would become more difficult.

The detective showed his badge to the guard at the barrier to the Senate complex then drove his car to the designated parking lot. He took several additional minutes seated in the car studying John Henry's report.

Shortly after that, he was inside the building. He worked his way through the tedium of the Senate's building security, showing his usual frustration at the process. The guard scrutinized the detective's ID. Thankfully, the detective had left his automatic in his desk but the guard still insisted he go through the metal detector.

'I haven't been told to make any exceptions,' he said, sounding like some recording.

115

Kovarik winced.

Two wrong turnings later, in the labyrinth that comprised the interior of the Congress building, and he was outside the senator's office. The doors stretched the entire height of the walls. He couldn't avoid thinking how pretentious they were and how they might reflect the occupant's vanity. His prejudices were oozing out of him.

Ever since his move from Baltimore several years before, he'd had difficulty embracing some of the culture of Washington, a black hole of political intrigue, a minefield of ambiguity where words had several meanings and promises had little currency. He loved his job but hated this aspect of the city, where rhetoric was the staple and honesty a rarity.

One of the senator's office staff politely acknowledged Kovarik's presence. 'Do have a seat, Lieutenant. He will be with you shortly,' said the young lady with a warm smile.

He murmured something that was inaudible. It wasn't meant to be heard. He continued to pace impatiently in the corridor outside, occasionally glancing through the doors into the office in search of any movement. After a long five minutes Kovarik was showing signs of meltdown, constantly peering into the office and murmuring a complaint. He turned quickly as the young staffer appeared again. 'He'll see you now, Lieutenant.'

This was the province of Dorman Forsyth, senator from a south-western state. It was obvious from the start that his manner was condescending and dismissive. 'I'm very busy, Lieutenant,' he said almost immediately, seated behind his large desk and shuffling papers apparently for effect. I did get your message and I don't wish to be unhelpful but I have a committee meeting shortly,' he said looking at his watch and forcing what was supposed to be some form of smile. 'I'm sure you understand.'

There was no reaction from Kovarik. He stared straight at the senator as if he hadn't heard a word. For those who knew the detective, it was a clear sign of annoyance.

The senator stood up from his desk. 'One of my staff would be only too pleased to speak to you,' he said waving in the general direction of his outer office.

The detective looked over his shoulder in the direction of the door. It was his turn to force a smile. 'That's good to know,' he added with an edge to his voice.

'Senator, let me make a few things clear here. Then there's no misunderstanding. I know only too well having lived in this city for several years, that words can mean different things to a lot of different people. Don't be confused. I don't do politico-speak.' He stopped, ensuring he had the senator's attention. 'You see, I'm not here to play those kinds of games. I do hope you understand,' he said, emphasising the words. 'I really don't care if you are inconvenienced, nor do I give a damn if you don't make your committee meeting, and I care even less if it has to wait while you answer my questions.' He stopped again and looked out into the outer office again, conscious that he was being overheard. 'Now I wouldn't want to embarrass you in front of your staff but that's up to you. That's your choice. If you prefer we can go down to the privacy of police headquarters

117

and have our conversation there.' He took a few moments to look about the office. 'It's not as plush as here but we have improved the accommodation in recent years and we will try to make you as comfortable as possible.' He gave Forsyth a few moments to assess the climate. He didn't think the senator would accept the invitation, no matter how gracefully it had been extended. But Kovarik was insistent and forceful. 'I'm here for some answers. You do understand?'

The senator looked uncomfortable and called to the outside office to close the door.

This time Kovarik accepted the invitation to sit down. 'I don't know what your business is with Professor Draper. We will discuss that in a moment. My immediate concern is his assault of which I'm sure you aware,' he said glancing at the *Washington Post* on the desk.

The senator fidgeted in his chair. His hands played nervously with a pen.

 Kovarik would like to have dragged the son-of-a-bitch screaming out of his comfort zone to the cold clinical forensic lab. There, to see the professor laid on a slab, colourless with his death mask and the smell the formaldehyde surrounding his pitiful lifeless corpse. The more he thought about it, the more attractive was the idea.

'I'm going to ask you one more time,' he said trying to subdue his inner feelings of contempt. Without waiting for a reply, he continued. 'If I don't get my answers, I have a room downtown which I reserve for those who need some encouragement to part

118

with the truth.' Kovarik didn't hold back. 'You would be surprised how inspirational a few hours in that environment can be.' He stopped, this time waiting for effect.

The senator's face had lost some of its previous colour.

Kovarik intended to drive the point home. 'It never ceases to surprise me. I don't suppose it should given its austerity.' He grinned.

The senator wasn't sure if the comment was meant to be funny or not. He tried to force a grin in return.

'I take it, senator, you're not too keen on that option?' commented Kovarik.

The senator leaned across his desk, flipped a switch and spoke.

'Julie, can you tell the committee, I'll be late. I don't know how long I'll be delayed.'

Kovarik nodded in approval.

CHAPTER 15

Hanya Smolka sat in her car on the Potomac quayside, watching the houseboat residents come and go. She slipped a pair of binoculars from its case, focused the distance control and homed in on the marina about two hundred yards away.

It was late morning, so the traffic to the fish market behind the parking lot had emptied of trucks and was beginning to be replenished by cars driven by shoppers on their way to buy the fresh produce or others who fancied lunch at the many restaurants on the riverfront.

She turned back to the passenger seat and to the file Krupin had given her.

He hadn't given her any orders or even hinted at what she should do. She knew what was expected. That was part of her training. Initiative and action were supposed to be the hallmarks of her profession; the trained intelligence gatherer, the analyst with acute observational skills, the undercover agent, the product of mother Russia, the patriot with unquestionable loyalty and the reliable foot soldier in the secret world which she now inhabited.

On first reading, the Krupin file had surprised her, especially when McCabe's name had been mentioned. Clearly, the journalist wasn't the same person she'd known so many years ago. Neither was she. They'd both travelled a long way since then and she'd often wondered how different her future would have been had she chosen another path. Those diverse options had presented themselves quite frequently over the years she had spent in the United States. She'd come to enjoy the culture so much and the freedoms that came with it. But she also knew it was easy to forget that her life there could be brought to an end in a second; an instant recall would have seen her back in Moscow. Then, where would she be and with what prospects?

She knew what Krupin and people like him suspected. They considered her a permanent defection risk. Given that, it had surprised her that she'd lasted, particularly in the soft job she'd enjoyed at the embassy. Perhaps she was the token hybrid; the patriot who was as charming as the Americans and just as attractive? Was that it; her role forever to be the Russian mannequin who was wheeled out on state occasions to sell her country's sophistication? But she knew the more she appeared immersed in the Americana lifestyle, the more she would be tested.

So, Krupin would have her watched and follow standard procedure. Unflinching loyal troopers would be his choice, the stupider the better. Select a couple who had unquestioning and blind loyalty, tell them that she was under suspicion, that they had been chosen as champions of the motherland, instruct them to monitor her every move and to report back to him. That was the way things worked. She didn't expect anything less. But she was no fool and she would make plans accordingly.

She opened the folder and smiled again at the photo of McCabe. Would he perhaps be greyer, more articulate, possibly more worldly and much wiser now? She looked at her face in the rear-view mirror. She still looked good but as she parted a little of her hair she could detect the odd strand of grey. She smiled at her vanity. How had the years taken their toll on him and did he ever have regrets and wonder what things may have been like had he taken a different route? She doubted he had any regrets. The young man she remembered was single-minded, passionate about what he did and could think of nothing but satisfying that calling. He hadn't changed much in one regard. She could say in all confidence; his pursuit of the story, whatever that might be, was still what drove him. This is why their paths had crossed again.

According to the Krupin file, he'd got involved in this through a man called Andy Gallagher, his supposed mentor and first editor. She bent over the seat and read his biog. She could almost hear the echoes of this man in McCabe. But he'd died recently and McCabe had picked up the reins, not knowing what he was doing or where he was going but following his news antennae. Clearly, he hadn't changed that much; if at all.

But the story outlined in the remainder of the file was vague. The atomic consignment had gone, been removed. A dozen men had been killed in the process. Why had the Americans been so reckless and where was the toxic cargo now?

Her equivalent in the US security services, primarily the CIA, would be playing their part; a classic cat and mouse game that seemed to have a mind of its own. She was confused and couldn't put the pieces together into any decipherable pattern.

What was she supposed to do? Was she expected to exploit the one-time relationship with McCabe and tag along behind him, in the hope that this human ferret would force the pace and she would be there to pick up the pieces? She didn't like that scenario for a host of reasons.

What about the professor who had the perfect cover with the veneer of respectable academia? How had he been involved? That's why she'd attempted to see him. But no such luck. His office had been empty and she'd left prematurely. Not for the first time had the CIA used academics to gather information to front research which had more than one purpose. It was well known that the Agency funded such projects in many grateful universities and colleges around the globe. Some of these clever teachers and researchers were Agency operators in their own right, feeding information to the Agency and their political paymasters. The authorities denied any such involvement but their involvement was real enough and their denial as predictable as it was false.

One of those power brokers on Capitol Hill was also highlighted in the Krupin file; Senator Dorman Forsyth, chairman of a Senate Committee on Homeland Security. What strings was he pulling and who was attached to the other end of that web? She could only guess.

She turned back to the quayside again and looked through her binoculars. She could identify McCabe's boat easily since a photo of it was contained in the file. She assumed that the figure on deck was McCabe but it was impossible to tell.

123

What was she to do? Wait until the journalist left the boat, so she could search inside and hope something came to light? She had no idea what she was looking for. That was the strategy she'd adopted with the professor; wait until his office was empty then see what she could find. But that hadn't worked. She'd been interrupted, probably by a student, before she'd had time to think. Then, the only option was to leave and quickly.

She spread out a copy of the *Washington Post* on the passenger seat. The professor's photo was given some prominence on the front page and the story was given a dramatic edge. It said he'd been surprised by an intruder, he had been seriously injured in what appeared to be a struggle but the police had no leads about the identity of the attacker or the motive. She expected limited information in the report but it did sound as if they had nothing to go on and the newspaper had printed a standard response. There were no quotes from the police.

Did that mean that the authorities were not commenting or really didn't know anything? However, what was definite was that the professor had been taken to hospital. The report did add that his injuries were believed to be serious. It wasn't her doing. He wasn't there when she was in his office. It could only have occurred after she'd gone. None of it made sense.

She looked through the binoculars again to the figure on deck.

He was wearing a pair of sunglasses and had put on a little weight but she wouldn't have had any difficulty recognising him.

She wondered if he would remember their time in Mosoow? If he did, what were those memories? That question was secondary. More importantly, what was she doing here? It didn't take much to work out that she was expected to rekindle an old friendship, and according to Krupin's inept moral compass, find out what he knew and, like the loyal comrade she was, pass the information up the chain.

In the process Krupin could test her loyalty. It would appear he couldn't lose. That equation sounded a little one-sided.

But she would dictate the timing and it would be on her terms. She wouldn't be railroaded into anything of Krupin's making. She turned the key in the ignition, put the car in gear and drove quietly out of the parking lot.

CHAPTER 16

McCabe watched the afternoon light disappear and the chill of the evening arrive in its place. The air felt damp and it was ready to rain. He shivered a little as he abandoned the deck and sought comfort in the warm lounge below. Through the windows he could see the cars in the park opposite on their way home, as their headlights flashed through the treeline.

He made himself some coffee, laced it with a capful of Black Label then settled at the desk. He took a drink of the coffee and decided he needed something a little neater. He poured himself a scotch and sat it beside his cup. He'd have both.

The *Washington Post* and some local newsletters gave him his first news of the attack on Draper. He was surprised, if not a little shocked. Did it confirm that whatever Andy Gallagher had been chasing was important to somebody and that the professor was part of it? Perhaps it was just a sad coincidence? None of the news outlets had any more information on what had happened. The web version of the local newsletter, primarily because of its immediacy, was the most current. They even had managed to corner the policeman in charge of the investigation, Lieutenant Pat Kovarik from DC Homicide, who wouldn't make any comment. That was no surprise. But there was no movement on the story.

McCabe had known the detective, almost since arriving in Washington. He liked the policeman. Not for the first time, they'd found themselves chasing the same rabbit, albeit from different directions.

They had even traded information, although those instances had been exceptional.

McCabe found such arrangements uncomfortable. The Press, the Fourth Estate, was meant to be at arms' length from anything that was Establishment. Also, it was supposed to make such authority accountable for its actions. It was his role, as a journalist, to stand independent of the police and its political overlords. That was the theory, taught to cub reporters and in journalism schools. The reality was less black and white.

Kovarik was equally reluctant to forge partnerships with the Press. He didn't have any high moral arguments to support his view. It was much simpler. He disliked the Press and didn't trust the journalists who fed its avaricious appetite for sensation. Any cooperation was done with reluctance and extreme caution. His goal was to catch villains. The journalist had other ambitions, namely to get a story. Rarely, he told his team, were these goals compatible.

McCabe chuckled as he read the report. He was certain of one thing. It wouldn't be long before the tight-lipped detective would discover he had visited Draper. It wouldn't be long before the detective came calling.

There was something about the *Washington Post* photo of Draper that he hadn't noticed before. Also, it was the same one he'd brought from Scotland. He peered at it closely. It was the background. Perhaps it was exaggerated when the newspaper

127

magnified and cropped the photo. The more he looked at it, the more he was certain. He fired up his laptop and tapped in a few commands. A screen full of text appeared and with it the photo he was seeking; the famous image of Dounreay, Britain's first home of atomic power.

 Who could forget the dome? It could be seen for miles, erected on an old airfield abandoned by the RAF at the end of the Second World War. It was here, just west of John O'Groats, at the tip of Scotland, where the UK took one of its first faltering footsteps into the world of fast breeder atomic power. The confidence of the reactor's creators and policymakers appeared shaky with their decision to build it at the end of a runway barely a hundred yards from the sea. There would be no sophisticated measures adopted in the event of an uncontrolled emergency. The solution would be crude and befitting the little they then knew about the forces they were about to unleash. Critical problems at the reactor would be solved immediately by dumping the entire structure into the North Sea; so said the legend.

 As the years progressed and they discovered how frighteningly little they knew of the forces they were playing with, it became obvious to the powerbrokers and scientists alike, that a maritime graveyard would be no solution if there was a serious emergency. It was just as well they'd never had to test the option.

 McCabe had been to Dounreay and Thurso, the nearest town, several years before to write a few articles. The workers had their local social club which was lively most weekends. Many of the young men went south, principally to Glasgow, to do apprenticeships and left what seemed like a disproportionate number of single girls at home. He had many happy memories of that social imbalance.

Things were much different now. Nearly fifty years on, the Dounreay atomic reactor still dominated the landscape and, while being decommissioned, it was the favoured site for any nuclear problem child. There, it was hoped, the refuse would remain safe from the instabilities of atomic physics and from the ambitions of those who sought to acquire it for their own destructive political ends.

McCabe took a deep breath and a mouthful of scotch. The photo begged the question. What was Draper doing there? He typed some more instructions into his computer. Apparently, there was a local newspaper called *The Caithness*. It hadn't existed when he'd visited more than twenty years before. A few editions contained fairly comprehensive reports about the latest load, delivered to the nuclear complex by the US. McCabe had two thoughts.

First, the reports were unduly detailed which seemed surprising, given the delivery was supposed to have occurred in secret.

Second, the more cynical might suggest there was something more behind this story. Somehow, it didn't feel right. It was obvious, even to the most inexperienced news hack, that someone wanted it to be known that this consignment had arrived at Dounreay.

129

That begged the questions: who and why?

Senator Forsyth was agitated. The visit from Kovarik had thrown him completely.

Had the detective witnessed the agitation, he would have been pleased.

A voice on the office intercom interrupted Forsyth's thoughts.

'The committee sent through a message, senator, wondering whether you will manage to attend? They're at a crucial decision about........'

She didn't have time to finish.

'Tell them I won't make it today, please continue without me,' he said, trying not to sound too sharp. He lay back in his chair reliving the conversation with the detective. It had gone poorly and he hadn't made a favourable impression on the policeman; if anything he'd made matters worse.

It was obvious Kovarik was aggressive and not a man who was easily susceptible to political pressure. Also, it was evident from his approach that he didn't trust politicians. He probably didn't trust anyone.

'I don't want to be disturbed,' Forsyth fired at the intercom, opening a drawer in his desk and extracting a leather-covered notebook. He flipped through the pages until he got to the one he wanted. He vacillated. Should he phone or not? He slammed the book shut and threw it back into the drawer.

The *Washington Post* still lay on his desk. It had been stupid to have it in front of him when the homicide detective had arrived.

Surely, reading the news of Draper's attack didn't mean anything? What could Kovarik conclude from that? His hands were sweating a little and his thinking was out of focus. He pulled open the drawer again and grabbed the leather notebook. He opened it at the page he'd read barely a minute before.

His finger ran down the listing and stopped beside Aiden Johns. He had second thoughts, third thoughts. He was still vacillating.

The visiting detective was shrewd. How much did he know that he hadn't disclosed?

Forsyth needed to make the call. The decision had taken him more than five minutes. He picked up the phone and started to dial. Half way through dialling, the intercom interrupted again. He abandoned the call. Perhaps it wasn't a good idea anyway?

'Senator,' said the quiet, calm and polite voice from the outer office.

'I told you I didn't want to be disturbed,' he shouted sharply. He regretted the outburst immediately. 'Sorry, Julie, I've got a bit of a headache.'

'Would you like me to tell your visitor to come back another time?'

'Visitor?'

'He said his name is Mike McCabe a journalist from a British newspaper, the *London Daily Herald*.'

The senator's face dropped. He recognised the name. He couldn't place it but it triggered something in his memory. 'Did he say what he wanted?' Forsyth didn't wait for any answer. 'Tell him I'm busy and I'll get back to him. Ask him if he'd like to submit his questions. Take a number where he can be reached.'

Where had he heard the name? Forsyth was struggling to remember. He turned on his computer and typed in the name. It didn't take the machine much time to respond. The screen filled with lines of rolling text, each article more interesting than the one before.

The journalist's exploits were well documented. Over a career that spanned nearly thirty years he'd gone from small-town newspaper reporter to international correspondent who'd rubbed shoulders with the high and the mighty across the globe. A few had been unhappy at his critical prose and expelled him, while others attempted to cultivate his obvious influence. His newspaper, as was to be expected, sang his praises. Others were more guarded. He was a great investigative reporter, almost all agreed, but some saw him as naive in his expectations of humanity. They wondered if anyone could live up to his code. However, it was evident he was a man with substantial strength of character. It was rumoured he'd once been recalled from the US by his editor in the face of a threat of expulsion. Now he remembered the name. It wasn't a rumour. The British journalist had ruffled a few influential feathers on Capitol Hill. They had threatened to withdraw his visa. His editor had defused the crisis and recalled him. It wasn't too long before he was back.

Forsyth knew he needed to solve this issue and bring it to a head. Whatever he did, it needed to be done with stealth. He pressed the intercom again. 'Is that journalist still with you?'

'No, sir; he's just left.'

'Did you get a phone number from him?'

'He gave us two; one is his cell phone and the other is a house phone, although he actually lives on a boat.'

'On a boat?'

'Apparently it's on the marina beside the fish market. I must have passed it a dozen times.'

'What else did he tell you? Did you ask him to leave his questions?'

She didn't answer immediately.

'Julie, did you hear me? Did you ask him to submit his questions?' he repeated.

The intercom came to life again. 'He said that you would know what it was about. He said he'd already spoken to Professor Draper.'

The senator switched off his intercom, let out a long sigh and leaned back in his chair.

CHAPTER 17

Kovarik ran through the index of the CCTV camera tapes. They didn't cover all the areas of the Georgetown University campus but a fair amount of the thoroughfares, the gates and an overview of some of the adjacent streets. Amongst the cameras used for security on campus and those for traffic surveillance, he might just get the information he wanted.

The forensic video expert had segregated the tapes into viewing order. 'I assume that the dates and the times that you gave me haven't changed?'

The detective nodded. 'I'm trying to identify the people who may have visited the professor who was attacked about two days ago.'

The video specialist checked the dates, the times and the location covered by each tape. 'Some of the later ones we might have difficulty seeing in any detail because of the poor light. Not all of the campus is well lit.'

'The ones I'm looking for should be. There was a CCTV focused on the clock tower where the office is located.'

'Good luck. I'll set it up for you and then leave you to it; any problems, just holler.'

Two hours later, he had identified a half dozen people he thought looked out of place. They either didn't look like students or professors. All of them had been on their own. He'd eliminated anyone not alone and anyone outside the two hour timeframe when they'd estimated the attack took place.

The forensic joined Kovarik for the final selection. 'I can identify three of those you've selected. One is a post-graduate student and two, believe it or not, are professors. Of the others, I have no clue.'

The detective read from the statement taken by John Henry from a student witness. *She was tall for a woman, I'd say, blonde and pretty. She had a baseball cap on, so I could only see part of her face.*

The detective focused the machine on one of the figures, tall, blonde with a baseball cap. It was very difficult to see any facial features but he was sure she was a prime candidate. 'Can you enhance the picture any,' asked Kovarik, hopefully.

The video expert shook his head. He didn't look optimistic. 'No it would be much too grainy for it to be any use to you. Identification would be impossible. At least we can tell it's a woman.'

'We knew that beforehand,' replied Kovarik bluntly. He stood up muttering to himself as he prepared to leave.

'But the news is not all bad detective. I have developed some really interesting facial identification software.'

'I thought you said you couldn't identify her?'

The expert nodded. 'Correct but I was wondering if we could pick her up in one of the other tapes?'

'So?'

'Those,' he said, pointing to the tapes from the CCTV in the adjoining streets.

Kovarik said nothing but still had a puzzled look on his face.

'There,' said the forensic pointing to the baseball capped figure walking across the screen.

'But we still can't see her face any clearer in this one,' sighed Kovarik. 'But thanks for trying,' he added, sounding frustrated.

'That's true but look at that,' said the specialist pointing to the screen. 'I can enhance that, no problem.'

The detective peered at the new image. 'What are you telling me?'

The expert laughed and seemed to rub his hands, like a teenager playing a computer game, as he pointed to a car on the video. 'She just got out of that,' he said smiling. 'It's not obvious now but, with a few adjustments, I'll be able to read the number plate without any difficulty.'

Several times John Henry had driven past the apartment block in Bethesda where their suspect lived. Her name was Hanya Smolka, Russian, tall, blonde and attractive. The car registration gave almost everything they needed to know about her, except why she'd been in the office of Professor Melvin Draper about the time he was attacked. The small blue Ford was a private registration on the vehicle database but a check through a few others gave a more comprehensive picture of the woman. She worked at the Russian Embassy but had been in and out of the USA over several years, studying at undergraduate and postgraduate level. Her credit rating was good, she had two American credit cards, a bank account and a regular income from the embassy. According to her credit profile, she leased her apartment with her own money, although as a supposed trade attaché she had other options, principally embassy accommodation provided by her employers.

John Henry parked the car after his latest circuit of the block. The van at the far end of the street was conspicuous and its inmates made no attempt to disguise their presence. They were quite visible in the front seats and were obviously watching the apartment block too. He dialled a number on his cell phone while watching the van carefully. 'It's a silver Dodge,' he said into the phone. 'I'll text the number plate.'

Kovarik, who'd arrived separately, edged his way along the sidewalk, tapped the rear window of the police car then jumped into the front passenger seat.

'She's left the building once, went to the grocery store at the corner and back,' said John Henry turning towards him. 'But something strange is going on here.' He leaned across the windscreen and pointed to the van on the opposite corner. 'That van and the two guys sitting in it haven't taken their eyes off this building since I've been here. When she went for a walk, they followed her.'

'She's a good looking gal,' said Kovarik. 'What do you expect?'

John Henry gave the detective a curious look. It was obvious he wasn't sure if Kovarik was joking. He decided to ignore the remark. 'They're watching her, I'm sure. And here's another thing. I ran a check on the van's plates. It belongs to the Russian Embassy.'

The detective looked puzzled. 'I thought you said...'

'She does,' interrupted John Henry. 'Yes, she works at the Russian Embassy.'

'Her own people have a tail on her?'

'That's about the size of it!'

Kovarik still looked puzzled. 'They don't trust her?'

John Henry shook his head. 'But she's a trusted comrade. That's why she's where she is,' he said quite confidently.

'So what's changed? Those goons have been sent by somebody,' said Kovarik, nodding towards the van.

'Clearly not everybody has bought her loyalty card, although they haven't made any secret of their presence, have they? You would need to be pretty short-sighted not to spot that pair.'

'I wonder if the show is not for her but someone else?' queried Kovarik. He knew Washington was awash with diverse political interests, from every nation in God's creation, where they watched each other in an endless cycle of cat-and-mouse.

'Whoever it is can't be too far away; probably in one of those buildings opposite. If it's one of ours, we may have a problem.'

John Henry shouldered his door open.

'Where are you going?' asked Kovarik, sounding surprised.

'I thought we were going to interview her.'

The detective thought for a moment. He knew interviewing had a methodology, the success of which varied from one occasion

138

to another. The subject was the variable, as was the crime but above all the timing. At the moment, it didn't feel right. He touched John Henry lightly on the arm. 'Let's leave it for now. I have a feeling we need to know more about this before we go barging in. I don't want her closing up shop on us.' He nodded again towards the parked van. 'Nor do we want those guys and the person who sent them to run for cover. Let's watch for a bit then take stock.'

 John Henry pulled the car door shut. He understood the logic.' I was thinking we might get the forensic team up here to do a scan.'

'For what?'

 The young policeman had learned over his years to tread carefully with Kovarik when pushing an idea, particularly one that had technology at the fore. The detective's years of experience provided uncanny insights into solving crimes. Discipline and old fashioned police-work were at its core, where science was a support not a substitute.

 On more than one occasion Kovarik had been frustrated with the progress of an investigation. Instinctively he knew the crime, the criminal and the motive but the science, he felt, held him hostage. If he couldn't prove it scientifically, he didn't have a case. Sometimes it appeared as if he believed the techniques were a hindrance not a help.

 'I'm sure you know all this, Lieutenant,' said John Henry, cautiously. 'But they have scanners which will detect any electronic equipment in that van.'

Kovarik was giving him his full attention.

John Henry, a little nervous, stumbled on. 'They also have the equipment to scan the buildings opposite her apartment,' he continued. 'Heat scanners that pick up body heat and even voices.'

'Although, if you wait long enough until Miss Smolka leaves in her car, they'll follow quickly enough. I don't think we need science for that. We're the detectors. It's called good police-work.' The Lieutenant smiled. 'But go ahead!'

John Henry expected more discussion but there was none. It took him by surprise. 'We might need a court order, if we're breaching privacy laws,' said John Henry slowly, waiting for the backlash.

Kovarik ignored the remark.

John Henry thought of repeating the comment but then decided otherwise. His boss had heard him well enough; repetition was just inviting trouble. He knew Kovarik was aware of the restrictions which the privacy laws imposed. He also knew the detective bent the rules because, unreservedly, his focus was catching criminals. Sometimes, things got in the way; they had to be circumvented.

On those occasions John Henry felt uncomfortable. But Kovarik was running the show and was willing to take the rap if it went wrong.

'Brief them properly before you get them down here. I don't want them scaring the rabbits.'

The detective's cell phone buzzed. 'Kovarik' he answered bluntly. 'Dead. Where? We'll be there.'

Kovarik stood on the sidewalk and stared at the car. To anyone passing, there appeared nothing out of the ordinary. The driver behind the wheel looked ready to start the engine. His left-hand was on the steering wheel, his other was dropped by his side, staring straight ahead. Had he the proper parking permit he might have sat there for days. Aiden Johns was dead alright. There was no dispute.

John Henry walked to the driver's door, slipped on a pair of white latex gloves and pulled at the handle. The body didn't move an inch but appeared rigidly glued to its driving position. Kovarik paced round the vehicle, read the number plate and the baseball bumper sticker then studied the body. 'Who found him,' he asked, inspecting the corpse even closer.

'Parking official; apparently tried to caution him about his illegal parking. And when he didn't get any response, he called the police.'

'No other details?' asked the detective, still peering at the body.

'That was it, although initially he thought the driver was ignoring him, so he gave him a warning and walked away.'

'Very charitable,' said Kovarik, with a sarcastic edge to the comment.

'It was nearly an hour before he came back, he said.'

'A proper saint,' the detective added with the same cynical tone.

John Henry tried not to respond to the comments but he was finding it hard. He forced a smile and ploughed on. 'He noticed he was in the same position and then he phoned us. A patrol-car was here fairly quickly.'

'How long has he been dead?'

'The forensics haven't got here yet, although I have put a call in,' he said quickly before Kovarik reacted. 'They will be here shortly,' he added confidently. 'If the parking attendant or whatever they call themselves these days is to be believed, he couldn't have been dead long.'

Kovarik leaned into the car and examined the wound in the back of his head. 'Gunshot; looks like an automatic, I'd say.'

John Henry nodded in agreement. 'Just one shot from behind him.'

Kovarik looked at the wound again and followed a line. He wound up the window. 'Probably it was open,' he said. 'What does that tell us?'

John Henry had anticipated the question. He'd learned to be as prepared as possible when dealing with the detective who expected instant answers to any question. 'It was professional, not a passing crime, he was waiting for him and he might have known him.'

'I'm not sure we can conclude all of that but certainly I'd guess it was not a random killing. It had a purpose, whatever the hell that means,' responded Kovarik, stepping back from the car and walking to the rear again. 'Who is he?' he asked quickly.

John Henry was ready for that too. 'The car is registered in the name of Aiden Johns.' The young policeman seemed to hesitate. 'If he's the driver, our records say he works for the CIA. I haven't checked the body for ID yet.'

'Do we have an address?'

John Henry nodded and checked his notebook. 'Takoma Park, Lieutenant; there is an apartment, leased in his name.'

'Get there before they bar us from getting in.' The detective's cynical tone had returned. 'His employers will soon have that place taped up like a Christmas parcel. We need to get in there before they do. Do you understand?' There didn't seem any compromise. That was the way he wanted it.

John Henry was hesitant, caution evident in his voice. 'Shouldn't we notify.......' He didn't have time to finish.

Kovarik glared at him. 'I told you what to do. Get on with it, quickly. This man was killed on our watch, in our precinct, in our jurisdiction. Do it! If you have any trouble, let me know.'

It was evident, there was to be no compromise.

John Henry looked uncomfortable. He suspected he was bending, if not breaking, some procedure but he knew Kovarik hated being pushed aside in an investigation, particularly by what he would call the faceless cloak and dagger brigade. The detective was well known for his dislike of those who operated in the shadows, some committing crimes in the name of national security.

But for the detective there was only one set of rules. Sometimes he seemed inflexible; a stance which caused him constant

143

trouble in Washington, a breeding ground for political subversion. More than once, he'd been reprimanded by superiors for his supposed inflexibility. He didn't see the bigger picture, they said. Kovarik, in his own way, would tell them where to put it. The Washington game of political fudge he neither played nor liked. Most of the time he coped and sometimes, like today, he was making a statement.

The forensic team arrived.

Kovarik stood on the sidewalk inspecting the street, the car and the traffic. They were barely a hundred yards from the main gate of the campus but it was a small side-street, well hidden from view. 'Perhaps he parked his car out of sight for a reason? Find out why he was here and we'll find out who killed him.' He walked around the car again.

John Henry said nothing but watched the detective intently.

One of the forensic team looked puzzled, as he left his colleagues and approached Kovarik. 'You said the body has just been found?'

Kovarik nodded. 'Dead a few hours, we thought.' He looked uneasy. He sensed a challenge.

The forensic shook his head. 'It is a gunshot wound alright but this man has been dead for more than a day, possibly longer.'

'How can that be?' asked Kovarik in disbelief.

'It's a quiet street. I suppose people just go about their business. How was he discovered?'

Kovarik shook his head. He looked annoyed and ignored the question. 'I want the car and the victim checked over thoroughly,' he said quickly then turned to John Henry 'See if you can find our victim in any of the video footage that we've gone through already when we were looking for the girl. Two murders this close together; can't be a coincidence. They're related somehow. I don't believe in coincidences. He was here for a reason. We need to find it.'

CHAPTER 18

Hanya Smolka drove onto the Potomac quayside again. This time she got out of the car without hesitation. She knew which boat she intended to visit. It had been described in detail in the file she'd been given by her Russian embassy boss. At first, the address surprised her. But on reflection, she supposed it would fit the personality which she once knew; the self-assured young man who, in his own parlance, would have been considered cocky.

The McCabe she had known ran with the pack but insisted on being free from it. His independence was almost obsessive. The file had said he'd married but, not too long into it, something went wrong. According to the same report, and how accurate the sources she wasn't sure, he had bought a houseboat in London in the aftermath of a messy divorce. Apparently, it had been an old coal barge and was now fitted out with the standard contemporary needs that would befit a modern man. The one he lived in here, a few hundred yards from where she now stood, had been rented from a friend. Obviously, McCabe had got the bug of living on the water.

The marina was busy with some boats being painted and repaired after the predictable severity of a Washington winter. Some boats were floating offices for architects, designers and all sorts of commerce. They generated busy customer traffic all day, unlike the residents who only emerged when pursuing some domestic chore or while they were coming or going.

The houseboat would suit McCabe's idea of independence, she thought, a floating commune away from the normality of the world which surrounded it. She'd watched his boat for more than an hour on her last visit to get a glimpse of the man she once knew, the man who was once a friend, the man who was once her lover. What personality that man now had was not described in her file. She suspected the reason was simple; they didn't know. It would be interesting for her to find out.

John Henry sat in his car on the street opposite the main parking lot on the Potomac quayside about a hundred yards from where his suspect had parked. To the left of the vehicle, at the far end of the lot out of immediate vision, was the van which, predictably, had followed the girl too. He didn't think the Russians had any inkling of his presence. He'd been particularly careful and had followed at a discreet distance.

The suspect walked confidently along the quayside towards one of the houseboats. The main gate to the pontoons had been left open by some workmen unloading materials for repairs. Within a few minutes, she stood beside one of the boats.

John Henry had been at this address before; so had Kovarik. But he didn't want to be the one to tell him. For the moment that could wait. He looked at his watch. Right now the Lieutenant would be checking on the success of the forensic team's surveillance. They'd responded immediately to his request about an hour ago and ran their checks. By now, with a bit of luck, they should have a result.

147

Kovarik was back at the forensic unit harassing the CCTV specialist.

'That was a great job you did for us on the surveillance video,' Kovarik said generously, complimenting the video expert. 'The license plate number gave us a name and address,' he said, actually sounding grateful.

The forensic was surprised; Kovarik's surly reputation had gone before him.

But this time, the detective's smile was genuine. 'I gather John Henry, who is more up to speed on your technology than I am, was confident that we could call on your assistance again. Did he speak to you?'

'We know John Henry well,' the technician said quickly. 'We like him a lot; a nice man.'

Kovarik nodded without any facial expression.

'He told us you had a subject under surveillance. That there was a van he thought was doing the same, possibly eavesdropping or video recording your suspect.'

'That's what we wanted to prove,' commented Kovarik bluntly.

The specialist seemed quite animated. 'I don't know if John Henry explained how the technology works.'

The Lieutenant didn't look enthusiastic at the idea. 'If you could just tell me the results,' he said curtly.

The technician ploughed on, regardless. 'I think it might help you understand the limitations of what we do, and those doing the surveillance, Lieutenant!'

Kovarik shrugged. He was the captive audience and had little choice but to listen.

The forensic allowed himself a modest victory smile. 'We were able to monitor the van for about ten minutes before they moved, with John Henry following. But it was enough. They emit signals when the equipment is operational, so detection was no problem. If they had been there long enough we could possibly have told you what type of equipment.'

'It doesn't matter, just that they were watching our suspect,' commented Kovarik bluntly.

The expert nodded. 'Most certainly they were. We have direction finders and the van was certainly focused on the apartment that John Henry had pinpointed. So were the other lot.'

'You were able to detect them too?'

'Oh yes, and that was much easier. We had more time too. A schoolboy could have followed their signals; eavesdropping equipment and full video gear. We had monitored the building first using thermal imaging.'

Kovarik looked restless again.

'Sorry, Lieutenant; didn't mean to bore you. Simply put, we can get an image emitted by body heat. Two guys sitting at a window looking through sophisticated video equipment mounted on a tripod is hardly a challenge. The glass can give us a bit of trouble; reflections. But not a problem we couldn't solve.'

Kovarik looked more attentive now. 'You found them and the apartment?'

149

'That was the easy bit.'

The detective reacted instantly. 'What's the difficult bit?'

The forensic smiled with satisfaction. He looked pleased he'd been asked the question. 'They're both armed and the equipment is top of the range surveillance electronics.'

'Which means?'

'Very expensive; not private sector; I'd guess government payroll most likely. Yes, that would be my guess.'

When the elevator stopped, Kovarik drew his automatic. By now John Henry had joined him and did the same. This was the floor identified by the forensic specialists. The third party clandestine eavesdropping team, they'd discovered, was three doors down. The detective quietly moved up one side of the corridor with John Henry covering the other.

They held their guns carefully in both hands, their eyes glued to the door about thirty feet away.

Kovarik stopped one side of the door and signalled to John Henry to move to the other. The detective listened at the door. There wasn't a sound. He tested the handle which seemed to turn easily. When it engaged to open, he shouldered it and fell into the apartment. He knelt on one knee with his gun pointed down the dimly lit entrance hall.

John Henry did the same, kneeling beside him.

They listened and after a moment rose and moved cautiously forward. They heard a voice from the lounge at the end of the hallway. There was a brief silence then the voice started again. It was incoherent. They couldn't make out what was being said.

Kovarik raised his gun higher and pushed it ahead of him. He kicked open the door then raced through it followed by John Henry.

The woman behind a vacuum cleaner screamed.

The policemen froze for a moment then instinctively separated checking the different rooms in the apartment. It was absolutely bare with no one in sight. There was no video and sound detecting equipment either, no sensors or telescopes on tripods; the birds had flown. Also, thanks to the lady with the vacuum cleaner, there was probably little evidence that anyone had been there at all.

'Where are the men?' asked Kovarik, looking at the cleaner. She looked bemused and shrugged her shoulders.

He wasn't sure if she understood. He tried again. 'The people who rented this apartment where are they?' he asked, as his voice level died away. He could tell from her expression that she didn't understand a word. He then tried to tell her to stop cleaning by waving his hand across the vacuum cleaner. In the end, he pulled its plug from the wall.

At that point she shrieked and ran out of the apartment.

Kovarik shook his head in despair. 'Get forensic up here but I suspect it's too late,' he said turning to John Henry.

'What the hell do you think you're doing?' asked an officious voice from the doorway. Whoever he was, he looked annoyed.

151

John Henry could see Kovarik ready to react but stepped in quickly. He showed his badge and introduced himself and the detective.

'I'm Mr. Cavell, the manager,' he said looking unimpressed at the badge and even less at the introduction. 'So that allows you to barge into this apartment, with guns, and scare my staff half to death?'

John Henry could see Kovarik ready to boil over. He knew the detective well enough to predict how he would react. Pompous officials brought out the worst in the detective. Before he could contain the situation, Kovarik had moved forward. It was too late. The genie was out of the bottle.

The Lieutenant was fighting his basic instincts. He wasn't going to waste time with preliminaries. 'Two men who rented an apartment from YOU,' he said emphasising the word. 'You could have committed a felony,' he added abruptly, without any qualification.

Cavell looked less pompous.

Kovarik could sense he had him on the back foot. 'At this stage we do not know your involvement,' he added with as much theatrical edge to his voice that he could manufacture. 'We like to keep an open mind,' he added generously.

John Henry could see the detective was having fun.

'I...I don't know what you're talking about, Lieutenant,' the manager stuttered, respectfully.

Kovarik walked towards the window and looked out into the street. He turned back to the manager. 'We have evidence to suggest that two men with electronic surveillance equipment have used this apartment to eavesdrop on residents in the apartment block opposite. You do appreciate that such activities would be a breach of US privacy laws and a criminal offence.'

The manager said nothing but looked shocked.

'It is possible that anyone who assisted them could be an accomplice?' added the Lieutenant, elaborating his point.

'We had no idea any criminal activity was going on,' responded the manager, using the plural, to ensure he solely wasn't carrying the blame.

'Our forensic people would like to inspect this apartment, if there is any evidence after your cleaner has been here,' complained Kovarik.

John Henry said nothing but felt slightly sorry for the unsuspecting Cavell.

'We'll be happy to give you every assistance Lieutenant,' responded the manager, sheepishly. The pompous posture of earlier had long gone.

Kovarik smiled and nodded in agreement.

CHAPTER 19

McCabe could see the Commodore, the dedicated manager of the marina, striding down the main pontoon, showing his usual excitement by waving his hands about while talking to himself. Who was going to be reprimanded today, McCabe wondered? It reminded him of detention and punishment at school. He hadn't checked out the neighbours as he'd promised, after his break-in. Perhaps the Commodore was waiting for some input so he could file his precious report?

It was obvious the Commodore was on a mission. His strides seemed to get more purposeful as they headed in McCabe's direction. He barely stopped at the gangway and, in seconds, was on his way up.

McCabe couldn't pretend he wasn't at home. It was too late; the door to the deck was open. He was still trying to think of something when the visitor climbed aboard, and was soon down the steps and into the lounge. What could he do but welcome the old chap?

'Nice to see you Commodore,' he said, unsure whether he was about to be scolded by the headmaster or not. 'I'm sorry, I didn't get back to you about the neighbours. I did forget that you had a report to write.' He tried to make it sound important, although he suspected he didn't sound too convincing.

The Commodore seemed to be thinking of something else. 'It's me that should apologise. I said that you would be back within ten minutes. She waited. I did offer her a drink of something but she said she couldn't wait any longer.'

McCabe felt as if he'd walked half way into a conversation. He was grasping at the threads to get some pattern. What the hell was he talking about? 'Commodore,' he said with laughter in his voice but clearly lost. 'I'm not quite following you. Could you slow down and start at the beginning. Who was she, when was that and what happened?'

'I saw you walk up the pontoon and along the quayside. Since you didn't go to your car, I thought you'd just gone for a bit of exercise.'

He'd actually taken a boat to the other side of the estuary. 'I went for a boat ride, Commodore, to try and get some things straight in my mind. I find it therapeutic. You were saying?'

'She came to visit but you were out. I suggested she wait in my office but....'

'Commodore, we've been down that road already. Who are we talking about?' McCabe sounded a little frustrated. He was tired of the confusing chit-chat.

'She left her cell phone number,' said the old man, handing over a small piece of paper.

McCabe took it and read the numbers. They didn't mean a thing. He sighed and looked at the Commodore. He'd just run out of patience.

'Hanya, that's what she said. Her name is Hanya Smolka.'

McCabe pressed the button on the elevator for the thirteenth floor of the National Press Building. Where the elevator stopped would be where he would meet her. Several decades gone, a lifetime ago and then one cell phone call later, they were to be together again. It seemed surreal.

He sat for ten minutes at the table reading the menu but nothing seemed to register. He could see the words in front of him well enough, imagine the cuisine, picture the dishes but his mind kept returning to one image; a young Russian girl in Red Square laughing at his juvenile jokes. He couldn't remember them; thank God for such mercies. He was constantly looking back at the entrance to the club restaurant.

Then she was there. He'd wondered whether he would remember her and what would be that memory; a girl barely out of her teens or just a picture contrived over the years? Whatever reservations he had of any memory disappeared in an instant. The tall, blonde beauty who stood at the door and was being directed towards his table was none other than the girl he'd met a lifetime ago.

He stood up as she arrived at the table, her glance seemingly as awkward as his. His mind was racing for the right words. He was supposed to be the wordsmith. What was the right greeting for someone who had meant so much, so long ago, and now appeared like a phantom out of his past? He said nothing, moved towards her and kissed her on one cheek.

She turned the other cheek towards him and smiled.

He kissed that too.

'You're taller than I remember,' she said quietly.

He laughed. 'So are you. Were we still growing when we first met?'

She laughed with him.

It seemed to break what ice was present.

'You've broadened out into......' she said, as she sat down in the chair opposite him. 'How should I describe you?' she teased.

'Mature, perhaps, but that's a little clichéd,' he said.

'You used to say that maturity was overrated.'

'Such wisdom in one so young; I don't remember saying anything of the sort.' He laughed again, sounding faintly nervous.

A waiter arrived at her elbow. She sat down and glanced quickly at the menu. 'I'll need a bit of time but in the meantime could you bring me a very cold glass of Chablis?'

'I'll join the lady, make that two,' responded McCabe. 'Every time I bring a guest here for lunch, I have to recommend the crab sandwich but the buffet is excellent too,' he added.

She said nothing as she took her time studying the menu.

As independent as ever, he thought.

The afternoon came and went with the lunch, the coffee and a few drinks afterwards. They talked about what they'd done in the time that had passed since they last had a meal together but he sensed it was all for show but for whom? He wasn't fooled by her credentials as a trade attaché at the Russian Embassy or that she'd suddenly appeared in his life without apparent reason. It didn't take much insight to determine she'd been encouraged to seek him out. The question he still had to answer was why?

Years ago in Moscow, she'd been trusted to rub shoulders with the Press and he'd been surprised how well she'd coped. The surprise dinner they'd had in a small family run restaurant off Red Square, all those years ago, had not been on the schedule. He'd realised, fairly quickly, that his bad grammar had caused the fortuitous error which gave them the tag of newlyweds. She didn't make any attempt at correction and she enjoyed what followed. The service was appalling but who was in a hurry? Before they could even place their order, a very large and middle-aged waitress was blatantly trying to sell them Dunhill International cigarettes and tins of caviar. Capitalism was alive and thriving even then, albeit underground.

By the end of the trip they'd become lovers. She'd asked nothing of him and had made it clear they would never see each other again. The promise made it easier for both of them. He never wrote anything which embarrassed her and he guessed that was her job well done. What they said to each other remained private, as did the meaning of the words they exchanged. They'd been together; that was no secret. Did she tell her superiors everything that had gone on, all the things that had been said, the intimacies of two young lovers? Clearly, her behaviour hadn't marred her record, or had it?

But now was the present in Washington. He'd put her into a cab when they'd finished lunch. Neither of them knew where it would or should go from there; perhaps nowhere. But, despite the rhetoric, she was still mother Russia's daughter and a loyal one too. Neither of them were fools. Their previous relationship was being used, so she could keep close to him; but why? Surely it couldn't be anything Andy Gallagher and his neurotic Georgetown Professor had uncovered? Not for the first time had he been used as a stalking horse as he stumbled, if not bumbled, his way through a story and in so doing made the waves which would bring the truth to the fore.

He saw her taxi disappear through the traffic lights on its way to Bethesda. Within seconds he produced his cell phone and called London.

He wondered how he would feel about asking Walker to run a check on *Hanya Smolka, Trade Attaché at the Russian Embassy, Washington, DC.*

When the phone was answered, he'd find out soon enough.

CHAPTER 20

The *Crab Tree* is one of the most popular restaurants on the marina-side of the Potomac. The seafood dinners are excellent and can't be rivalled by any other establishment at twice the price. It is on the water's edge, so for McCabe, the ambience was second to none.

In normal circumstances, there was a substantial waiting list for a table. But McCabe knew the owner well and on many occasions he'd stayed late to share a few generous glasses of whisky. Needless to say, getting a table for dinner was never a problem.

Hanya Smolka sat opposite, looking even more stunning than she'd done the day before at lunch. She'd ordered a martini and he a straight scotch.

He'd managed not only to get a booking at short notice but to secure one of the nicest tables in the restaurant, tucked away in a small alcove with a large window overlooking the river. The faint lighting on the outside patio reflected off the water, giving it a ghostly effect. It appeared as if they were totally alone.

'I asked you why you'd suddenly appeared again in my life,' he said quietly. 'But you never gave me a straight answer.'

'Now, Mike, you know that's not true,' she responded with her broad charming smile.

McCabe was playing with her and she knew it. He was convinced that while she may have been westernised and allowed certain liberties, mixing with the Press was not one, unless officially sanctioned. It was difficult to be so cynical when facing her across the table in such surroundings. She would make any healthy-blooded male weak at the knees; a cliché but damn true.

She'd spoken a lot at lunch but in essence disclosed nothing. She'd told him about being in Washington for several years as a trade attaché, advising her government on US trade policy, but somehow, convincing though she was, he didn't buy it. He would love to have believed her. When they'd first met, he probably would have had fewer reservations but his experience since then exacted a price. He didn't want to push her; she would make her own decisions in her own time.

She was assessing him as much as he was her. 'Did you ever get married, Mike?' she asked. It wasn't a subject he wanted to dwell on, never mind discuss. The marriage had been good but he'd screwed it badly, obsessed with work as only an ambitious young man can be. But in the end, he was away too long and too often. Not surprisingly, she'd found solace elsewhere. In his profession it was commonplace, as were the excuses. He'd taken it all for granted. One day the marriage was no longer. 'Yes but it ended badly.'

'What does that mean; a messy divorce?'

He was getting slightly irritated. He didn't want to go down that road but it seemed inevitable, given her questions. Why did he have the feeling she knew the answer? 'No but it was painful.'

'Do you miss her?' she asked, almost in a whisper.

161

It was the first time he'd been asked that question. He hadn't even asked it of himself. He wasn't prepared to discuss the matter any further. There was no point. There was nothing he could share with her. He had another swig of his drink. 'I think I'll leave it there,' he said, quite bluntly.

It was as if they were getting to know each other for the first time. This was going to be a slow process and perhaps more difficult than he'd first thought. Why be in a hurry?

'What about you?' he asked with no real purpose other than to change the subject.

She shrugged. 'I thought we weren't going to talk about that subject,' she responded quickly. She seemed to realise her answer was curt. 'It was a bit of a disaster, as you would say in the west. It didn't work out.'

'Why?' he asked instinctively.

'He wasn't always like that. It's an old story. He changed or something changed him.'

'What?' he asked in reflex again. He couldn't help it.

She looked serious. She wasn't going any further.

He really didn't care or even want to know the details. The conversation had moved on, except in one respect. 'I still don't know why you've suddenly reappeared in my life,' he persisted.

'I thought I'd answered that,' she said with another charming smile. 'I'd seen your face in one of the diplomatic newsletters a few months ago and I promised myself I'd look you up. I thought I'd explained that?'

She had told him before. Now he'd heard the same story repeated. It was word perfect, a flawless retelling. But he didn't believe a word. At the moment he didn't care.

He raised his glass and accepted her answers at face value, for the moment. But that acceptance was as superficial as her answer. He still hadn't decided where she was coming from and where he would fit into her equation. She was on a mission, of that he had no doubt. His initial feelings were mixed, if not confused. She was an extremely attractive woman with whom he'd had a previous relationship and still held in some affection, but she was in Washington under license from one of the most repressive and secretive societies on earth. By definition, she was a loyal comrade; he had to keep telling himself. Much as he would have loved, particularly in this setting, to wave away any misgivings, he couldn't convince himself that her appearance had been a coincidence. He was still at a loss to determine precisely what she'd been assigned to do and what part he would play. That made her appearance all the more disturbing. Obviously, she knew more than he did.

Was her interest in what Andy Gallagher had discovered? Or was it totally unrelated? He refused to believe that the timing of her appearance was coincidental. The papers he'd brought back from Scotland had, apparently, been worth stealing. But so what? They'd meant nothing to him and the Georgetown professor, from whom he'd sought some enlightenment, was tight-lipped. The academic's nervousness would seem to

163

confirm that McCabe had touched on something. Could that be what the lovely Hanya was chasing too?

After his second talk with the Commodore, he had made a few belated enquiries of his neighbours. As he'd suspected, no one else had seen the thieves who broke into his boat but, more significantly, there had been no other break-ins. Not that he was a scholar on such matters but he would have thought the thieves would have tried their luck elsewhere. For whatever reason, they'd targeted his boat in search of something in particular.

He had to assume that, whatever it was that Andy Gallagher and Melvin Draper had uncovered, was the Russian's target too. Could he also suppose it was they who were responsible for his burglary? Was Hanya plan B?

Whoever these interested parties were, it looked as if they thought he knew more than he did. It wasn't the first time he'd taken advantage of that erroneous assumption. In time, whoever they were, would have to show their hands or give him some clue. He would have to be ready to exploit that edge.

However, none of that helped him with Hanya Smolka. She still confused him. In their adventure in Moscow, without any reason being given, she hadn't appeared at the final Press meeting. It had left him thinking the worst. The same torturous questions kept repeating themselves for months. Had he put her in danger or, more painfully, was what they had between them just been a ruse, ordered by her superiors?

For all he knew, that could be the case now. But he didn't care. He was going to enjoy every minute of it.

164

McCabe was on deck savouring a cup from the first batch of the morning's fresh coffee. He was up surprisingly early, given the night which had gone before. It hadn't been raucous or out of hand, merely long and indulgent.

The food had been excellent. The servings of crab and the garnishing were enough to give a satisfied inner glow to anyone who enjoyed good food which, blended with a couple of bottles of superb wine, could only produce an effect that was positively ecstatic.

Inevitably it could only encourage more excess. The liqueurs followed and then the night-cap; in her case, predictably, vodka; in his, scotch.

He looked at his watch. It was barely six o'clock. He watched the cars begin to stream their way through the park opposite; the early office-bound commuters trying to beat the traffic and get their much sought-after parking spots. The headlights flashing through the trees and the lingering mist hanging over the estuary, as always, gave it a haunting sensation.

He had another mouthful of the coffee. He was tempted to lace it with a capful of Black Label. He looked at his watch again. Even for him it was a bit early. He walked back to the staircase leading down into the lounge. Nothing stirred; she was still asleep.

He could convince himself that he didn't know what happened. But he did. They were consenting adults. Had he been just going to have another night-cap and then phone her a cab or was that

165

never on the agenda? There had been no resistance on either side.

McCabe's cell phone rang. Somehow in the silence it sounded louder than normal.

It was Walker. 'Hope I haven't woken you too early but this is the only chance I have of talking to you. I'm busy the rest of the day.'

McCabe laughed.

Walker probably had a small interval in which he could visit his latest conquest, undoubtedly while her husband went about his daily chores. In that short timeslot he would do his best for the struggling marriage; so admirable! 'Not too many would make your sacrifices,' McCabe chuckled.

'It's a difficult job I have to do this day,' responded Walker. 'You should try it McCabe. You've probably forgotten what it's like to get laid.'

'To the matter in hand,' replied McCabe sounding serious. 'But don't tell me how difficult it has been to get the information. If you haven't managed to get anything just say so and we'll leave it at that, OK?'

'That'll be the day,' Walker said quickly. 'But it was difficult this time, as it happens. The clever thing about getting information is not to let them know how you got it. Just like a cat-burglar.'

McCabe shook his head. He'd heard the boast before. Walker liked the theatrical but was still the best in the business in discovering secrets, caches of data supposedly protected by all sorts of methods; safes, electronic firewalls, confidential agreements. He still was able to circumvent most safeguards.

'She went to Harvard and Georgetown Universities when she came to the US, would you believe? She's a very clever girl; an impressive linguist and political analyst. She strikes me as the sort of girl you should settled down with, McCabe. I did expect her to look like one of those burly women in Russian hotels who looked after your room keys. You know the type? They look as if they could pull a plough single-handed. And probably carry the horse at the same time. They probably did.'

'Let's move on,' interrupted McCabe.

'But the photos I have of her; well she's delightful. You couldn't pull her McCabe; definitely too good for you.' Walker was having his fun, again at McCabe's expense.

'She wouldn't appeal to you. She's not married.'

Walker's voice sounded a little more serious now. 'It wasn't always that way, I'm led to believe. '

'It didn't work out. I know all about that.'

'Really?' responded Walker, sounding surprised. So you know about the abuse, the domestic violence. It makes pretty sick reading. He sounds like a real asshole. Nice to know it's not just the civilized west which breed such cretins.'

'When was it?'

'I don't know. But she's out of it now. She managed to get stateside. I have a feeling she must have had some political influence somewhere.'

'Political influence?' repeated McCabe.

167

'Mike, you know what that means. She pulled strings, came stateside for a new life and got it. She graduated, MBA Harvard and Masters in Political Science at Georgetown. She was still part of the embassy staff, even when she attended school. She'd been in the USA about three years; business, commerce and trade are her forte.'

McCabe made a few mental notes. 'That doesn't tell me what she's up to now.'

The line went silent for a moment. 'No it doesn't. I have a few feelers out. We'll see what emerges. But the word is that the Russians are really concerned about what the Yanks are up to.'

'Stop talking in riddles, Stan.'

'The consignment of nuclear fuel the Americans took from Georgia; Georgia USSR , that is or was. They don't know where it is.'

'I thought you said the Americans took it?'

'They were supposed to take it to Dounreay.........'

'In Scotland?' interrupted McCabe, looking puzzled. 'But they did; didn't they?'

Walker sounded irritated. 'I told you before. My sources said that what they delivered there wasn't Kosher.'

McCabe shook his head in obvious frustration. 'What the hell does that mean?'

Walker was sounding frustrated too. 'I don't know. I told you about the spillage.' He stopped talking for a moment and sighed. 'All I'm saying is, there's something wrong. The Yanks are not saying anything and the Russians are getting paranoid.'

McCabe could hear footsteps on the stairs from the lounge below.

'Oh, before I go. One interesting item,' continued Walker. McCabe was half listening. He could hear her getting to the top of the stairs.

'She was married; not quite sure if she's divorced. It's a bit vague. Hitched to some heavyweight Russian, in political terms that is,' added Walker quickly. 'She sounds a bit too sophisticated for you, McCabe,' he teased and laughed at his joke.

McCabe wanted to ask more, but before he could she was standing beside him. 'Sorry, got to go,' he said immediately and pressed the red button.

'Checking up on me?' she asked, still accompanied by her smile.

McCabe was caught. He didn't know how to react. By the time he'd thought about what to say, the moment had gone.

'While you were on the phone, I had a call telling me somebody has been making waves, checking me out,' she said quite candidly. 'Close your mouth, McCabe. Don't look so surprised,' she said, turning to go back down the stairs to the lounge. 'I need some of that coffee,' she added, nodding towards the cup he was holding. She stopped as she got to the top of the stairwell. 'Don't be embarrassed, my people ran the same checks on you.'

'What would they do if they knew you had been with me last night?' he asked, almost hesitantly.

She laughed out loud. He could hear it echo all along the quayside, in the quiet early morning. 'Why don't you ask them,' she said, pointing to the white van in the marina parking lot about three hundred yards away. 'I'm not sure if their eavesdropping equipment works efficiently over water.'

He stared at her. He wasn't sure if she was joking or not. She didn't seem to care, either way.

This time there was no hesitation. He pressed the call button on his cell phone. The police unit that patrolled the quayside was only a few hundred yards away. 'Good, morning sir. I don't know if the marina manager reported that I'd been burgled the other day. Nothing was stolen, from what I could see. But I wanted to report a suspicious looking van ....'

CHAPTER 21

John Henry, diligently and meticulously, waded through the CCTV tapes.

Kovarik was definitely correct. If Johns had been on the campus before his death, it might determine who he had visited. It might also indicate why he was there and, more importantly, why he was murdered. They were convinced there was a Draper connection.

Unfortunately, it meant going over all the tapes which had already been scrutinized and while it had been the detective's idea to revisit the CCTV recordings, John Henry knew of old how touchy things could get if it proved something had been missed in the original inspection.

It was a long shot that Johns had been to see Draper. But he agreed with Kovarik. Two deaths in such proximity were stretching coincidence too far. There had to be a link.

But the task wasn't as simple as it would at first appear. Once, it would have been easy to spot those on campus who were not students or faculty but no longer. Hundreds of people walked through the grounds by the hour. The university was on the tourist circuit because of the historic nature of Georgetown. There were the religious visitors, who wished to see the home of one of the first Jesuit communities to arrive from Europe. And there were the waves of prospective students, who dreamed of studying one day in one of the oldest academic institutions in America.

However, John Henry was determined to have a go.

Two hours later, they had some answers but it gave them no idea if Johns had visited the murdered professor or why he had been a murder victim himself. They did confirm that he had been on campus in the vicinity of the professor's office but nothing more.

'Could you run the same checks you did for the Lieutenant?' asked John Henry to the forensic video specialist who had, yet again, volunteered his valuable expertise.

'Like what?'

John Henry thought for a moment, to try and make his instructions and intentions as clear as possible. 'Can we use your clever software again that compared figures on the campus CCTV images to those on the tapes from the adjacent streets?'

'To find what?' queried the technician. 'It has limitations.'

John Henry gave one of his characteristic charming and disarming smiles. 'I'm a little ahead of myself. I wanted to see if we could do what you did before but do it in reverse.'

The technician interrupted quickly. 'I'm not sure we'll get clear enough images to identify a figure from the street. We were lucky with the girl. She was wearing a baseball hat and was tall, well above the crowd. But we can try.'

'I have another thought,' said John Henry. 'What about using the time on the video as the crucial control element?'

'You mean every figure in the video within the estimated timeframe of Draper's death, in the proximity of the office and in the streets outside?'

John Henry nodded.

'That's a hell of a tall order; before we had the girl's height and her baseball cap,' said the video specialist shaking his head. So, you want to match those who were near the office and then in the area of the adjacent streets at the approximate time of Draper's murder? Now THAT IS a long shot,' said the technician emphasising the words. 'A HELL OF A LONG SHOT.' He shook his head again. 'Give me an hour. In the meantime, why don't you go and have a cup of our dreadful coffee?'

John Henry did as instructed. He felt he was behaving like the Lieutenant, impatiently looking at his watch every few minutes. It was an hour exactly when he walked back into the forensic lab hoping they had some result. It showed in his face. 'Any joy?'

The forensic pointed to the screen. 'That's your man, the murder victim in the car,' he said confidently. 'He was on the campus near the office at the time you gave me, our approximate time of Draper's death. We can identify the girl, what's her name...?'

'Hanya Smolka,' replied John Henry quickly.

'Yes her, followed by the murder victim. But look at this,' said the video technician, pressing a few buttons and bringing up another picture on screen. 'Just before either of them was on campus, near the clock tower where Draper's office is, that

173

figure came and went,' said the forensic pointing to the screen again. He typed in a few more instructions then looked at the blurred image on one of the street CCTV recordings. 'That's the same man again getting into a black Mercedes. The time matches. That made three who had visited Draper.'

'Can we get a clearer picture to help identify him?'

'I'm confident I can but it'll take time. I can magnify it and minimise the distortion. I will let you know as soon as I have one. However, I want you to look at this,' he said bringing up a new image on the screen. 'While I was testing the program, I checked out any person who had been to see Draper in the last week, manually filtering out students and known faculty from the results. There was only one person who stood out, who clearly was neither student nor faculty. I don't know if it helps you but the image is amazingly clear.'

John Henry looked at the figure on the screen and sighed. There was no doubt. He would recognise the figure anywhere. 'I know him,' he said quietly, almost reluctantly.

'That's good news then, is it not?'

John Henry shook his head slowly. The figure of Mike McCabe near a crime scene was not good news, nor was the prospect of having to tell Kovarik. His cell phone rang. He turned to the forensic at the end of the call. 'I have to go. Do let me know as soon as you get a clear picture of the third person. I'll be in the market for some good news and damn soon.'

CHAPTER 22

Half an hour later John Henry pulled his car up outside a small house in Takoma Park. This was where Aiden Johns had registered his car and, presumably, this was where he lived? The victim, although murder had yet to be officially confirmed, wasn't an enthusiastic gardener. The front lawn and the bushes which lined the property were growing without any defined shape or obvious discipline. Just as nature intended, thought John Henry.

Kovarik was already on the sidewalk, pacing up and down looking at his watch. He didn't appear to be in any mood for the late-comer's explanation.

John Henry wasn't sure if he should even try. He shrugged his shoulders in apology. 'I've been with the forensics. The CCTV came up with a few interesting findings. They'll get back to me to confirm.'

'I don't need any confirmation regarding what killed this victim. He didn't commit suicide by shooting himself through the back of the head and making the gun disappear. It's who killed him I'm interested in,' ranted Kovarik. He seemed on edge. He pulled out his automatic, nodded towards the door and took a few steps forward.

John Henry did likewise, positioning himself on the opposite side.

The detective held his gun in his right hand then turned the handle with the other, giving the door a nudge with his shoulder. It slowly swung open with a slight creak. He pushed it further with his foot then slipped through the doorway quietly, followed by John Henry. They crouched with their guns held tightly in both hands. They remained still in the hallway's semi-darkness, getting used to the light then carefully edged their way towards the door at the end. They followed the same routine on this door then slipped into the lounge. It was in a mess; the contents of the cupboards and drawers turned out onto the floor. Somebody had been looking for something and in a hurry.

'You did tell me to get here first,' said John Henry, attempting to be humorous.

Kovarik didn't look amused. 'This wasn't Agency work. We've got a third party here. Life has just got a little more complicated.'

Together they checked the remaining rooms carefully. On both levels the chaos was the same. The kitchen and the bathroom hadn't been spared. They had got the same frantic treatment.

'Get forensic!' ordered Kovarik, as he holstered his automatic. 'If we're lucky we might get some prints. But I doubt it. I'll be in the coffee shop opposite. When you talk to them, ask them for an update on their CCTV check,' he added showing his usual impatience.

John Henry obediently nodded with a smile.

Kovarik sat at the far end of the coffee shop trying to devise some pattern from the few clues they'd managed to uncover. Perhaps none of these pieces were related at all? Two murders within a few hundred yards of each other were not natural occurrences. Nor did he believe in coincidences. But they were connected in some way; of that he was sure. Every detective instinct, honed over many years, told him so. Perhaps the same person committed both murders? Washington was no stranger to spurious and motiveless murders and assaults. But these were neither. They were deliberate, if not planned. Judging by the professor's office and the Agency man's house, the assailant was looking for something, an item he was prepared to kill to get. Then there was the Russian dimension; a glamorous member of the trade delegation at the Embassy who appeared to visit the murdered professor's office but who clearly was being stalked by her own people. None of those pieces fitted into any decipherable pattern. And why was the CIA researcher involved? No matter how he fitted the bits together, no shape emerged. John Henry would have more to add.

From the office shop, the detective could see that the forensic team had arrived at Johns' house and was being instructed by John Henry.

The young policeman pointed in the direction of Kovarik then left the forensics to examine the house. A few minutes later he was ordering his own coffee and another for Kovarik. 'I assumed you would like another, Lieutenant?' he said as he put the extra cup on the table.

177

Kovarik said nothing but pulled the fresh coffee towards him.
'I've been trying to recognise some pattern, something that links
what we know, but not with much success; any ideas?'

John Henry relished the rare opportunity to give his views. Too
often he felt in the shadow of the great man. He wasn't
complaining. The Lieutenant was highly experienced and
successful in what he did. He knew he couldn't get a better
mentor, although he sometimes felt that the detective's style was
a little too abrasive and his approach unnecessarily aggressive.
He preferred a more tactful strategy, one that was often the
opposite to that of his boss. But Kovarik had superb instincts
which did not always endear him to those who wanted a more
measured approach. On some occasions, the detective was
almost in conflict with those who insisted that forensics be given
more significance.

'There's too much reliance on science in these investigations,'
was one of the detective's much repeated philosophies. 'We're
policemen, who use science as a tool. But it's our job to catch
the criminals. Don't forget it.'

It was no surprise then, that John Henry introduced forensic
evidence with caution.

'Lieutenant, I've gone through the CCTV tapes again,' he said
as a preamble, while he watched Kovarik carefully.

The detective did nothing, just stared at him as he delved into
his new cup of coffee.

'Johns, our dead Agency man, was on campus,' added John
Henry. 'We can't confirm from the videos whether he was in the

professor's office or not but fingerprint checks might determine that, if we're lucky. If that was the case, I believe he was there to see the professor; for what reason we don't know. The Russian girl, Hanya Smolka, I'll bet was on the same errand. We can ask her for her fingerprints.'

Kovarik shook his head. 'She'll probably claim diplomatic immunity, remember, officially she's a delegate of the Russian Embassy. We have to be careful how we proceed there.' Kovarik had another searching look through the window, checking on the activity among the forensic team. 'Is that it?'

John Henry thought of explaining his logic and how he'd surmised that Johns' murderer might be on the tapes too. He suspected Kovarik would get too impatient. Perhaps he should wait and give him the results and his conclusions later? But he had to move forward whatever the risk. 'We have an image of a figure on the tape who could be Aiden Johns' assailant,' he said, eventually. 'Perhaps the professor's killer.'

'Could be?'

'He was caught on the CCTV outside the campus gates, near Johns' car.'

'Not much to go on, is it?'

John Henry was determined to plough on. 'He was also caught in the vicinity of Draper's office, before and after the professor's death.'

'Where does that take us? We have a figure we can't identify who was in the vicinity of two murders. Is that meant to be helpful?'

179

John Henry said nothing.

'Our job is to clarify; to separate the relevant from the meaningless.' The detective thought for a moment. 'What did he do when he left the campus, your unidentified figure?'

John Henry knew the question was coming. Unfortunately he didn't have a satisfactory answer. He had to tell Kovarik straight. There was no other way. 'He got into a car but we didn't get the number plate. We could try and pick it up in traffic cameras. All we know is, it was a black Mercedes.'

Kovarik finished the last of his coffee then had another check through the window at the forensic team's progress. 'So, correct me if I get any of this wrong. We have three possible killers, or witnesses to Draper's death or at least the circumstances surrounding it. One is dead, one we can't identify and the other may well play a diplomatic card. Is that right?'

John Henry reluctantly nodded. He was still struggling as to how to introduce his discovery of Mike McCabe. He could only guess the Lieutenant's response to that news.

'Judging by your silence, I take it that I got it right?' Kovarik shook his head in disbelief and made another visual check on the forensic team. 'Where would we be without science?' It didn't sound like a compliment.

John Henry looked uncomfortable, not because of the information he'd already disclosed but what had yet to come. He'd thought about how to say this a dozen times. But there was no other way forward. It was a bitter pill and he was still unsure how Kovarik would react. 'The journalist, Mike McCabe,' he said quickly, watching the detective carefully. 'I know you have had dealings with him before,' added the young man, choosing his words carefully. He knew his boss and the journalist had crossed paths on more than one occasion. The circumstances had varied and the atmosphere on those occasions somewhat mixed. He suspected there was a mutual respect between them but he also knew that Kovarik was no lover of the Press; he instinctively disliked them and distrusted them even more.

'The Russian girl went to see him on his houseboat the day we followed her,' he said quickly, like a bitter pill he had to swallow, trying to avoid its predictable and unpleasant taste. 'I didn't want to say until I could explain.'

Kovarik didn't react at all for a moment. But it was evident his mind was racing. He stared ahead and his eyebrows pulled together, as if he was focusing on some distant image, analysing his options. He looked disturbed.

John Henry went for broke. 'He's also on one of the campus CCTV videos. It looks as if he went to see Professor Draper the day before he was murdered. He is spotted coming and going in the vicinity of Draper's office. The timings are on the recordings but we have no other information.'

Kovarik didn't say a word in response. He stood up and walked out of the shop in silence.

CHAPTER 23

Senator Dorman Forsyth cornered the Commodore on the
quayside.

Normally, the marina manager was suspicious of anyone who
wasn't a resident but on this occasion his defences were down;
he was immediately star-struck. 'Senator,' he said almost in awe
of the visitor. 'I've been an admirer of yours for so many years,'
he said drooling, without any hint of embarrassment. 'I don't
think we've ever had someone like you come to visit the marina,
at least not since I've been here,' he continued. 'How can I
help?'

The Congressman looked awkward. He'd thought how to justify
why he was there several times over the last day and just as
many times on the drive that morning from Capitol Hill. He
knew the strategy was flawed. It was much more than that; it
was extremely hazardous. If it went wrong it could do more
harm than good.

So, why was he here?

The answer was plain enough and didn't need a political genius
to work it out. Mike McCabe, an investigative journalist of some
reputation, had gone to see Draper and then came knocking on
his door. He knew something.

The journalist had arrived in the wake of a gruelling and
disturbing visit from the DC Homicide police. Kovarik, the
visiting detective, was far from subtle. Perhaps it had been the

policeman's strategy, one that was meant to make the interviewee uncomfortable. It had succeeded.

Since the detective's visit, he'd gone over their conversation a dozen times, emphasising what he'd said and imagining the way he should have responded to some of the questions. In reality, he hadn't done very well.

Then the journalist turned up. McCabe had let it be known he'd seen Draper. It was meant to have an effect. This was no casual visit. It had a clear purpose.

Now, on the quayside, Forsyth was nervous and it showed.

'Yes, Mr. McCabe lives in the one with the blue paint, over there,' said the Commodore pointing in the direction of the houseboat at the end of the pontoon. 'I'll take you down there myself.'

'That won't be necessary,' said Forsyth immediately. He was still trying to decide how he was going to tackle this visit. He could hardly just turn up, claiming he'd been in the neighbourhood. If he didn't handle this with some care, he might find it exploding in his face. His very presence here might incriminate him. It could easily be implied this wasn't their first meeting, given that the journalist had been signed in as a visitor to his office barely a day or so earlier. The senator was vacillating again.

The Commodore smiled. 'It's my pleasure, sir. You would have trouble getting through the security gates unless I come with you.'

The senator nodded. 'Of course,' he said in compliance but he was obviously uncomfortable.

They walked together, along the main quayside to the entrance to the pontoon, the residents' gateway. Forsyth looked relieved when the Commodore left him alone after opening the gate. He walked towards the houseboats but seemed to hesitate as he got to the gangway opposite McCabe's. He looked as if he was having second thoughts again. It was too late.

'Senator Forsyth,' boomed a voice slightly above him on the houseboat.

Mike McCabe stood on the deck, drinking from a cup. 'I saw you a few minutes ago, being shepherded by our trusted Commodore. Did he bend your ear a little?' He laughed out loud.

The senator still looked uncomfortable.

'Come aboard, I can offer you a cup. I've just made a fresh pot.'

The formalities done, McCabe sat opposite Forsyth in the lounge of the houseboat. 'This is an unusual circumstance, Senator,' he said casually. It was an understatement.

The journalist's instincts were on alert. There was no doubt in his mind that the senator was here on a fishing trip. The catch was information. He wasn't quite sure of the bait. Again, McCabe might find himself pretending he knew more than he did. It was a plan that could easily backfire but he had little choice.

Draper's murder had been confirmed but judging by the press reports, no one, not even the police, seemed to be making any headway. The senator had some professional links with the professor but that meant nothing. McCabe was fishing too. That was the nature of his business; some roads led to somewhere, the majority did not. Unfortunately, he had to waste time going down a few dead-ends before he found out.

There was one fundamental question. What was the relationship, if any, that existed between Draper and Forsyth, or indeed his friend Andy Gallagher for that matter? The fact that the senator was seated in front of him suggested the relationship had some significance and was far from casual. That should tell him something.

Forsyth didn't respond to McCabe's comment. He looked a little more assured now but still cautious. 'I was quite shocked when I heard about Professor Draper's death,' he said, sounding genuinely concerned. 'I barely knew him. We had only spoken on a few occasions.'

That was another mistake, thought McCabe. His first was being here, the second was this admission of ignorance; neither sat well with McCabe. He was well-versed in the innuendos of political rhetoric and its ambiguities. Despite his decades in journalism, it always surprised him how blatant and obvious was political bullshit. Was he really expected to believe that this busy senator, who had a personal schedule busier than a train timetable, would turn up on his doorstep without purpose? It was obvious something concerned the congressman and he was anxious to discover what McCabe might know. That was the only reason he was here.

McCabe had also to find out the same from him.

McCabe had a number of ways to proceed but the results were all unpredictable. He could pretend he knew nothing and fumble his way through a mind game and see what came out the other end. Or he could use what little he knew to prod and question the senator. He would start with the obvious. 'Who do you think would want to attack the professor?'

The question didn't seem to bother Forsyth. It was clear he was prepared. 'I've been asked that a few times,' he said confidently. 'How did you answer?' fired McCabe immediately, trying to push him and give some direction to the conversation. The more he pressed Forsyth, taking him out of his comfort zone, the better. At least that was the theory.

But the congressman was a highly experienced combatant. He'd been in this arena before. Whatever Forsyth's intentions, at some stage McCabe would have to push hard for any answers. The senator wasn't on a social call or here to engage in idle chatter. He had his own agenda.

'Before the death was announced, I also spoke with the police.'

'Who was that?'

Forsyth sat further back in the chair. 'A very pushy Lieutenant from DC Homicide Police.'

McCabe smiled to himself. He didn't need a name. It was Kovarik with his distinctively overt and aggressive style. It didn't take much to imagine how the detective had reacted to the senator. The Lieutenant wouldn't take any prisoners. McCabe sympathised. They had much in common.

It was now time for him to get pushy. 'Tell me about those occasions when Professor Draper sought your counsel,' asked McCabe, intentionally loading the question.

'It was not advice. It was just information.'

'What kind of information?'

The congressman seemed to tire of the word game. 'Mr. McCabe, you came to me initially; how can I help you?'

McCabe wanted to ask him a similar question; why was he here? But if he did, he sensed he would get a wave of politico-speak and they would be going round in circles. Instead, he would settle for the full frontal attack. 'A close friend of mine in the UK was buried a week or so ago. He was a journalist but above all, he was a great human being. He never lied, or cheated or did the things of which we mortals are all too frequently guilty.'

The senator looked apprehensive, as if he was expecting some revelation, an exposure of an embarrassing weak moment for which he was about to pay a price.

McCabe felt the senator's unease. He enjoyed the thought but had much more important issues to address. 'He taught me everything I know professionally. Apart from integrity, he was hugely tenacious. Pursuing stories was his life, exposing that which others would seek to conceal was his passion.'

187

The congressman fidgeted even more, and made another attempt to get comfortable in his chair. He was getting visibly agitated.

'According to his phone records, he called Professor Draper, the day before he died. In fact, he'd called him several times over the week before.'

'How did it happen, his death?' interrupted the senator, sounding genuinely concerned.

'It's not important,' answered McCabe dismissively, conscious that the conversation might be diverted. 'It was considered an accident. What is much more important is that apart from speaking to Draper at a conference, he had an intimate dinner with a contact of his here in Washington.'

Forsyth mouthed a few words but nothing was forthcoming.

McCabe was unable to determine whether the Congressman was asking a question or making a statement.

'It took place at *The Mayflower*,' continued McCabe. He stayed silent for a moment. He was being dramatic and playing for effect. 'Now senator; we both know who his dinner partner was, so let's take it from there'.

Senator Forsyth pushed his cup across the table. 'I think I'd like another before we continue.'

McCabe poured a fresh one, handed it to the congressman and was back on the sofa.

There is some information which is privileged here, some classified and some highly confidential,' said the senator. 'Do you understand?'

McCabe was immediately on his guard. It was not the first time that he heard similar political overtures. It was easy to be impressed by the rhetoric and to be convinced that what was about to be disclosed was of some substance. It might be, but he would determine its currency. It was also the classic subterfuge, an easy smokescreen behind which any covert activity could disappear. If McCabe wasn't careful, he knew, the congressman would use the ploy to halt any further investigation. In the process, he would also tell him nothing.

McCabe was well prepared. He'd checked out the senator's biog before he'd gone to visit him. He was Chairman of a relatively new congressional forum, the Committee for Homeland Security. The US Congress website was comprehensive in its description of the committee, its membership and its goals. Its clout was unclear, as were any demarcation lines which existed between it and the security agencies. Congress had insisted on the oversight of the security agencies since the abuses of the Nixon Administration, which reputedly used the agencies to breach numerous privacy boundaries and spy on American citizens. Legislation was put in place in the wake of those scandals, but since the twin towers attack the reins had been slackened with too many politicos prepared to look the other way in the name of national security.

McCabe also knew that in the wrong hands and unbridled, such license could easily be misused.

'It's a question of national security,' said Forsyth, predictably. McCabe said nothing and just stared at the congressman. Was this going to be a game of poker or chess? He suspected both. But again, he was going to insist on keeping the conversation on track. 'Before that congressman, tell me why you were at the conference at *The Mayflower*? I thought the delegates were focused on energy?'

'Yes, in all its aspects; energy, nuclear, medicine, its entire spectrum.'

McCabe was pushing. 'Where did Andy Gallagher come into that equation?' he asked bluntly. 'As I said earlier, I knew him well and I know he was after a story. I would like to know what it was and I can only assume that you were part of it.'

The senator thought for a moment.

McCabe wasn't going to give him any more leeway. He wanted to maintain the momentum. 'I think it may have caused his death, accidental though the car crash may have been.'

The senator appeared thrown by the comment. Whether he didn't anticipate it or was unnerved by the tone, it was evident he was disturbed. 'Mr. Gallagher and the professor had a theory. It wasn't even that. It was a hypothesis. One of the questions like *what if*?'

'Which was?'

Forsyth seemed to anticipate the question. He relaxed a little. 'I'm afraid that enters the realm of national security,' he said again.

McCabe had expected that the reaction too. They'd left the chess game. It was now poker rules.

There was an obvious connection between Draper and Gallagher. Additionally, there was a relationship between Forsyth and the professor. Was there a relationship or connection between all three? Could that be at the heart of the story? He only had one card to play. If the game was poker he had to play it. But he must do it with conviction.

'Yes, I know it is,' he said almost nonchalantly.

Forsyth said nothing. He looked as if he wasn't sure how to respond. 'You do?' he said hesitantly.

McCabe had on his best poker face. 'I know about Dounreay,' he said without hesitation. 'I think we should talk about that, don't you?'

It was a great card to play but the game ended somewhat prematurely.

The senator rose from the sofa, crossed the lounge and had climbed the stairs on his way off the boat in a matter of seconds. He hadn't disclosed anything but in a way he had told McCabe all he wanted to know.

CHAPTER 24

Kovarik pulled up next to the patrol cars of the marina police. It was their expertise that kept this part of the Potomac quayside secure; a relatively small force by the standards of most urban precincts but highly effective.

The waterfront had changed character since Washington had become the US capital. From its early days as a swamp, it had graduated in stature. This particular part of the river had been transformed dramatically.

In the Civil War, it had been a demarcation point for Union troops, had been then the site of a major military hospital and, before its current transition, a successful port for commercial traffic. Fish, and the produce from harvesting the Potomac, was a regular trade on the quayside. The local fish market, which still exists today, has its roots in that history.

But the most dramatic urban change took place in the fifties. Previously, dozens of poor families had lived in basic river crafts on the water. The urban transformation which began not long after the Second World War was to be one of the biggest urban redevelopment projects in the USA. Buildings were flattened, including many churches with impressive historic ties, to be replaced by a new vista of modern living. Curiously, in the process, the residents changed in character too. Once the province of the poor, the waterside became much more affluent, its population living in houseboats equipped with all the trappings of modern comfort, a far cry from the basic dwellings of previous decades. Those who were members of the new nautical community were not only more financially secure than their predecessors but they expected more out of life than the daily fight for survival; the lot of those who'd gone before.

'Are you sure,' asked Kovarik, looking at the small building at the end of the parking lot.

'Yes,' said John Henry from the passenger seat. 'I know the sergeant here and I put in a call to him, after we spoke about McCabe.'

Kovarik didn't look relaxed. 'Why?' he fired back quickly.

'You remember the white van outside the Russian girl's apartment, the one we had Forensic check?' he asked, not entirely happy with the way the words had emerged. It sounded as if he was calling the detective to account.

The Lieutenant didn't react immediately. Someone walking along the quayside with a fishing rod had caught his attention.

'Yes, I do,' he said suddenly. 'I remember the white van. So?'

'I wanted to know if the police here had seen anything unusual.' He opened the door and began to walk towards the small building.

'And?' asked Kovarik, impatiently, following him.

'No, but they did caution the drivers of the van.'

'Why?'

'Apparently, one of the residents in the marina reported them.'

'For what?'

'I don't know the details.'

They reached the small building in less than a minute. It smelled of fish, like everywhere else on the quayside.

'Pat Kovarik!' shouted a very large uniformed policeman behind the main desk.

The Lieutenant smiled and shook the outstretched hand.

John Henry looked surprised. 'You know each other?'

The uniform laughed out loud. 'How are you Pat?' he asked Kovarik.

John Henry nodded. 'I guess I should have known.'

The uniform turned to John Henry. 'Your boss patrolled the waterfront in Baltimore with me for many years.'

'They were good days but a long time ago,' added Kovarik.

'You've got a good man there Pat,' said the sergeant, nodding towards John Henry.

The young man looked slightly embarrassed.

'I've checked on what you asked me,' the sergeant added. 'It was two of my colleagues who dealt with it. But I've talked to them and read their report.'

'There was something unusual then?' asked John Henry.

The uniform flipped through the pages of a ledger on his desk in front of him. He stopped, ran an index finger down a page then read the entry. 'A call about suspicious behaviour of the inmates of a white van, parked opposite the marina.'

'Suspicious?' queried John Henry.

The sergeant laughed aloud again. 'Some people get a bit jittery when they see cars they don't recognise or vans with no markings. Most of the commercial vehicles that come here are

194

for the fish market and have the names of the traders on the side. If they don't have and they hang about too long, people get nervous.'

'What happened?'

'We went along and checked them out. At first they claimed they were lost then they said they were just taking in the sights of the waterfront. They were asked to get out of the vehicle.'

'Why?'

'The two young patrolmen are relatively new and very enthusiastic. When they checked the inside of the van they found what looked like electronic equipment of some sort. They didn't know what it was but it looked suspicious.'

'Did they say why they were there?'

'They didn't give any more information?'

'The patrolmen checked their IDs.'

'Russian,' said Kovarik and John Henry simultaneously.

The sergeant shook his head. 'No, no; they were Brits.'

'What?' asked John Henry. 'Are you sure?'

The sergeant didn't respond to the question. He looked offended. 'We couldn't charge them with anything. It's not a crime to hang about the waterfront, even if you look suspicious and have a van loaded with electronics. They did check the number plates; rented at Washington Dulles Airport.'

John Henry looked puzzled. 'Couldn't be.'

'We do our job here very well,' insisted the sergeant. He still looked offended.

'Sorry, sorry,' apologised John Henry. 'But can I ask what colour was the van?'

The sergeant checked the ledger again. 'Light blue.'

'What happened to the white one,' asked John Henry, sounding frustrated.

'It was light blue,' repeated the sergeant. 'I don't know anything about any white van. The people we picked up were in a blue one.'

John Henry looked even more puzzled.

Kovarik had kept silent. 'Who reported them?' he asked suddenly.

The sergeant pointed to John Henry. 'Your clever young colleague here had been asking about the same man; a British journalist called Mike McCabe. He called the police. According to the marina manager, Mr. McCabe had a break-in the other day. Perhaps he was frightened of a repeat. Or maybe it's just a coincidence.'

Kovarik looked at the sergeant then at John Henry. 'I don't believe in coincidences; not this one, not ever.'

'Nevertheless, if you're going to visit him, you'll need to get through the security gate. I'll speak to the Commodore,' said the sergeant picking up his phone. 'He's the marina manager. That's what everyone calls him. There's a long story in there but I won't bore you with it.'

Five minutes later the Commodore was escorting them through the security gates. 'Mr. McCabe is a very popular man this morning,' commented the Commodore.

'Really!' replied Kovarik, more by instinct than with any genuine interest.

'Are you here about the burglary?' asked the Commodore. 'Mr. McCabe said there was nothing missing.' He leaned into the policemen and lowered his voice to a whisper. 'I don't think he was being entirely straight with me. He probably didn't want to cause a fuss; that's his style. But I think what he said wasn't true. He did look concerned.'

'When was that,' asked John Henry.

'A few days ago when he'd just come back from the UK. But that was probably just a coincidence.'

Kovarik shook his head then looked at John Henry. He didn't need to say what he was thinking. 'What did you mean when you said Mr. McCabe was popular this morning?'

'I'm afraid who visits our residents is a private matter,' said the Commodore, sounding a little superior.

Kovarik glared at him.

John Henry winced. He knew what was coming and was poised to say something. Again, he was too late.

Kovarik's response was as predictable as it was blunt. 'We have cells full of people who refuse to cooperate with the police.'

The Commodore's face drained. 'I didn't mean that I wouldn't help the police, Lieutenant. It's just that there is a certain amount of confidentiality attached to my position here.' He looked shaken.

Kovarik didn't say anything. He just stared which added another layer to the tension.

'Senator Dorman Forsyth,' the Commodore disclosed without any more resistance.

 The detective brushed passed him without making any further comment. He turned to John Henry. 'I think we need to pull some of these strands together. Go and see the Russian girl. I'll tackle it this end.'

CHAPTER 25

John Henry was impressed when he entered the elevator of the luxury block in Bethesda. The carpet in the hallway entrance and the ones inside the elevator were soft and spotless. Even the piped music was high quality. It seemed a strange place to have a stereo system. He was surprised how anyone on an average income could afford to live in such splendour. It was obvious Hanya Smolka wasn't average.

Barely making a sound, the elevator came to a halt on the top floor. John Henry could imagine what the view would be like from one of the apartments on the outer side of the building. He was about to find out.

The file on the Russian had grown into a substantial dossier now, with pages on her background, education and status at the embassy. The power structure in such diplomatic circles was not something with which he was familiar. Kovarik, being an old-fashioned cop, discouraged his team from being captivated by any such privilege.

The diplomats, or anyone attached to the dozens of embassies in Washington, were a world unto themselves. They lived in splendour but immersed in a curious schizophrenic existence, representing their own culture while trying to comprehend and woo one totally different. Some were immensely successful while others returned home after years of frustration and failure. There was no ready formula which many found out the hard way. The Russian girl, supposedly a trade attaché of undisclosed rank but with immense influence, appeared to be one of the success stories and invaluable to her employers.

John Henry opened her file on his cellphone. Her linguistic skills were envied by many and it was this talent that had guaranteed her success in the USA. She had no trace of her Russian origins and spoke with a slight East-Coast American accent, cultivated in part by her attendance at two of America's finest centres of learning, Harvard and Georgetown. They don't come any better, he thought. An MBA from Harvard would open many a door for someone of lesser personal attributes. He scrolled through the electronic file on his phone. Even with the limited quality of the photo they had managed to obtain, it was clear that Comrade Smolka had beauty as well as brains. It was unclear why she had been chosen for the post in Washington, or what clout or rank she had within that diplomatic circle, but she was an important player in the Russian game. What the connection was between Mike McCabe, the hard-drinking, foot-in-the-door journalist from the UK, and this smooth Russian beauty was disclosed nowhere in the file.

The forensic team had made some headway on the CCTV footage he'd trawled with them. The fuzzy pictures of the unidentified man, whom they had culled from the videos as a possible witness or suspect in the professor's murder, were much clearer now.

Not for the first time had he used his contacts in other departments and accessed their databases to identify suspects.

Sometimes it could prove difficult, opening him up to accusations of breach of privacy. But he was prepared to take that risk. He needed to identify the man in the video. If the suspect wasn't on their database, there was every chance he'd just entered the US.

'No question at all,' said his contact in Immigration. 'He's a big fish. I suspect he's watched wherever he goes, although he entered the US with a diplomatic passport. His name is Colonel Nikita Solokov. He's KGB, unquestionably. The FBI or the CIA, I'll bet, are pretty familiar with this guy. But you don't want to get involved with the likes of him. These people play rough. I don't have access to all his pedigree but what I have read makes me very cautious. He's accredited with being the man they bring in when other methods have failed. Killing would appear to be no obstacle.'

'What would be so important to bring the likes of him to the table?' asked John Henry, hoping the contact could offer some guidance.

'I don't know. His employers obviously think so. Sorry, that states the obvious. But be careful. As I've said, they play for keeps. You don't want to find yourself on the wrong side of this man.'

John Henry had every intention of heeding the advice. However, he knew Kovarik wouldn't take a back seat and let the security agencies dictate the play. Crimes committed on his patch, and on his watch, were his responsibility to solve; that was the detective's philosophy.

John Henry wasn't going to be the man to tell him otherwise. He stepped out of the elevator.

The carpeting in the corridor was just as plush as before, as were the fittings and wallpaper. He checked his cellphone and read off the address. Two more doors up on the left he stopped and rang the bell.

John Henry didn't hear a sound until the door opened slowly. He didn't think her photo did her justice.

Hanya Smolka stood in the doorway.

'I rang earlier, I'm........' started John Henry with his badge flipped open.

'I guessed as much,' she said and offered a hand in greetings. 'Do come in,' she said closing the door behind him. 'Can I get you something to drink? It's a little muggy today.'

'No thank you,' he said, as he walked ahead of her into the lounge. He stopped at the entrance, as if waiting to be seated by a maitre d' at some top-class restaurant.

She laughed and gestured towards the sofa. 'Please, do sit down? Did you say you wanted something drink?'

'OK. Water would be fine,' he said, making himself comfortable on the sofa.

She disappeared into what looked like the kitchen and a few seconds later reappeared with a bottle of water in each hand. 'I'll join you.'

They were ice-cold. He felt the relief as he drank. 'Thank you.'

She sat on a large leather chair opposite. 'You know I could plead diplomatic immunity?' she said, appearing very serious.

John Henry looked at little awkward.

'But I won't,' she added quickly. 'Glad to be of help.'

He looked relieved. In truth, he'd thought about that as a possibility, after Kovarik's warning. Initially, he hadn't taken it seriously but then had made a few enquiries. He was cautioned to tread carefully. Had she decided to shelter behind the immunity, he wasn't sure what he would do. In theory, she couldn't be charged with any crime. And while his enquiries were light years from that possibility, he was also told that legally she couldn't be questioned about possible criminal intent or involvement. Just to add another layer of uncertainty to the scenario, if she didn't invoke immunity, it still didn't give him complete license. He'd been warned several times to be careful. With that said, he felt he would get nowhere if he allowed such limitations to be imposed on his conversation with her. He wasn't going to be intimidated or feel inhibited.

He was also in a dilemma. What could he disclose? He couldn't tell her that she had been identified at the scene of a murder, or that she was a suspect, and had been under surveillance since they'd discovered her on a CCTV videotape. But he also knew she was smart and could deduce from his questions how much he knew. He felt a little nervous.

'Miss Smolka,' He hesitated for a moment. 'Can I call you that?' She smiled graciously. 'Of course.'

He smiled in return. 'Do you know a Professor Draper?' he asked cautiously, pulling out his notebook and pen.

There was no attempt by her at fudge or denial.

'From Georgetown University? The poor man who was murdered the other day? I read about it in the *Washington Post*.'

'That's him,' he said softly. His style was the opposite to that of Kovarik. He disliked aggressive confrontation but preferred, instead, to extract information by charm, or at least with subtlety. It didn't always work, as the Lieutenant frequently reminded him and also demonstrated. However, it was his first port of call.

She held nothing back. She was as straightforward, frank and as quick as her profile had outlined. 'Yes, I went to talk to him, or at least that was the plan but I didn't,' she said bluntly. 'You know that, otherwise you would not be here. You no doubt spotted me on the CCTV which seems to be standard on every US campus now?' She had spotted the cameras as she'd walked across the lawn and into the main building. Anyone with a brain would have seen them. He also knew it was only certain individuals who would be looking for them.

But John Henry was taken aback by her candour. There was still no attempt at denial.

'And you are here, to check on me,' she said slowly while sipping her water. 'Am I a murder suspect?'

However, she'd chosen her words very carefully. 'You said you didn't talk to him,' he said, reading from his notes. 'Did you see him?'

She looked at him very carefully, as if she was pondering some issue. There was obviously some inner conflict. The answer to his question, for her, was not easy or instinctive. 'I'm sorry, I cannot say any more.'

John Henry, even with his charm, was also tenacious. 'I could be left to assume that you didn't speak to him because he was already dead.' He could feel her getting tense.

She moved in her chair, as if to get more comfortable. 'I would be cautious about rushing to any conclusion,' she said then smiled. 'Don't Americans have the right not to incriminate themselves? I'm sure you extend that same courtesy to visitors too?' She was playing with him and she felt he knew it. But she wasn't going to admit seeing Draper's dead body. She hadn't. He may well have been on the floor, behind his desk. She didn't know. The office was poorly lit and she was in and out in seconds. Even if she had seen him, it would be stupid to admit it. It would have put her at a murder scene and that would mean testimony. She wasn't going down that road.

'You are not being accused of anything and you have your rights like any other. But keeping vital evidence from the police is an offence in itself,' he said and watched her for effect. 'But, of course, I suspect you know that. Could I ask you what you went to see Professor Draper about?'

She stood up; a gesture which said the interview was over. Her smile was back. 'I'm sorry, I cannot say anymore,' she repeated. 'I think we're done,' she added quietly.

He responded to the signal and walked to the door. Just before he got there he turned towards her while pulling out his cellphone.

The forensic team and their magic software had done an excellent job. The quality of the picture, which had been enhanced, was impressive and even with untrained eyes, Solokov was easily recognisable.

John Henry pressed a few buttons, inspected the photo on display and handed the phone to her. 'Do you recognise this man?' he said while watching her reaction. 'We believe he was on campus, about the same time as you, visiting Professor Draper.'

She moved closer to the picture. The smile disappeared in an instant, as she inspected the photo. 'Where did you get this?' she asked, obviously disturbed.

John Henry took the phone from her but said nothing. Her reaction told him much. The picture was of no stranger and no friend. As he turned to close the door behind him, she still looked in shock. He didn't see the view from her windows after all.

CHAPTER 26

McCabe ordered a double Black Label and found himself a seat in a quiet corner of the Press Club lounge. He sat back, jingled the ice cubes in the bottom of the glass and thought about the session he'd had with Forsyth.

There was nothing too surprising about their meeting, although turning up at the houseboat unannounced was unprecedented. It was obvious he wanted a discreet venue and his goal was to find out what McCabe knew. That was ironic, because the journalist wasn't sure what he knew either.

What he had was the usual jumble of pieces that appeared to be connected, but after various attempts, they still didn't show any decipherable pattern. It wasn't for the first time that he'd been down that road; following a scent that ended nowhere, or trying to force ill-fitting pieces into some sort of pattern that wouldn't bond. On those occasions the remedy was simple; go back to basics.

The story obviously started much earlier, but for him it had to be Andy Gallagher. His one-time mentor had been actively following a story. If he had reached any conclusion, it wasn't written down anywhere in his house, although it could just as easily have been in his head awaiting his dated typewriter.

But what McCabe did know was not insignificant. There was a connection between Gallagher and the Georgetown professor. Was the something they shared sufficient reason for the professor to be murdered and what was the link between the dead man and the nervous senator?

The conversation with Forsyth was a classic verbal contest between journalist and politician. The former rarely gave ground, hoping to bait the interviewee reluctantly into some admission without disclosing what he knew already. The politician would predictably fence verbally, stretching the meaning of words to the limit, but in the end disclosing nothing. The contents were not an entire waste of time. Invariably, they exposed the parties' interests.

But in this case, the two combatants were old campaigners. McCabe had no intention of making any concessions. He wanted straight answers to equally direct questions. But that was never going to happen. In turn, the congressional committee chairman had disclosed nothing while probing for information. In the end it was a stand-off.

To McCabe, it was obvious he was on the right track.

Forsyth was ruffled· His cautious questions and evasive answers told that story.

McCabe had another swig of his scotch. It was going down too quickly and much too easily. It was barely lunchtime. He still had a day's work ahead of him. He walked to the bar, finished the whisky then ordered a chicken club-sandwich and a large coffee. No more booze. He had to try and keep a clear head, or at least think clearly. The coffee arrived promptly. He took it, sat down and began the analysis again.

On reflection, not all was lost. The senator could have been spooked by what was said. He may even have got what he came for; a confirmation of what McCabe knew or didn't know. But it was obvious the mention of Dounreay triggered something. It had been a gamble, a bluff that suggested he knew more than he did. But it had a dramatic effect on Forsyth and the interview, if that's what it was, had ended abruptly.

McCabe could speculate forever on that subject. What Gallagher and the professor had come across, he was convinced, was more than a theory, that much was confirmed. Forsyth wasn't concerned about some theory arrived at in the small hours of an academic conference, fuelled by a good dinner and too much brandy. Whatever it was, it was real, certainly to the congressman, to the dead professor and to Andy Gallagher. That too was a fair bet. But the rest of the detail was vague. Clearly, the atomic reactor site in Scotland was a vital clue. But that didn't tell him anything he didn't know already. The real clue would be in answer to the obvious question: why?

It didn't take a genius to conclude that it was not the physics that concerned the senator. There were serious political dimensions to this story. Forsyth's interest confirmed that much. But McCabe could spend hours speculating on it without result. In the background were the Russians whose attentions added another confusing layer.

McCabe finished his coffee quickly. Oh hell, he'd have another scotch. It was lunchtime.

Andrei Krupin read the directive which he'd received from Moscow. The content didn't surprise him but the tone certainly did. Unquestionably, it was the result of one filed to his superiors by Solokov, with the intention of discrediting him and spreading venom where it could do the most harm.

Krupin was caught off-guard and felt under siege. He needed some effective strategy, without which the play would be dictated by his vindictive visitor. He lit another Sobranie; the third in half an hour. He felt he was boxed in, unable to control the situation. If he didn't do something, the momentum would overtake him.

Clearly, Moscow was unhappy or they would not have even considered a third party who was meant to deliver the results which so far hadn't materialised. Though why this security hard-man, of all people, had been given such freedom in Washington, he found incomprehensible.

But Washington was a town where actions had huge political ramifications. They were reported, analysed and dissected by the world press. It was no place for the crass skills of Solokov. He reread the Moscow directive. Clearly, they did not share his view. According to the memo not enough cooperation had been given to Solokov and if his mission was a failure, Krupin would be held directly responsible.

He read it once again, getting angrier and more annoyed with every reading. The blame could not be placed at anyone's door except his own. He hadn't seen it coming and he was experienced and smart enough to have predicted it. It was a classic manoeuvre of Solokov, who had been trained in every form of subterfuge, but also had cultivated an effective amoral and unscrupulous toolkit on which he could draw at will. 'Asshole,' he shouted aloud then had another long drag of his cigarette. Despite numerous unsuccessful scans of his office, he was still convinced there would be some bug picking up anything he said. 'Asshole,' he shouted even louder. He hoped they were listening. He felt a victim. Was he so paranoid?

He spread a copy of the *Washington Post* on his desk. The murder of the Georgetown physics professor was given front-page prominence. The police still said they knew nothing. He flipped to a small item on the inside page. There they reported the mysterious death of a young man, discovered in a car on the precincts of the university. There was no reported connection. Perhaps they didn't know.

Krupin did. He was in no doubt; it was the crude and reckless handiwork of Colonel Nikita Solokov. He finished the Sobranie, extinguished it in his ashtray and immediately lit another. He needed to do something and quickly.

CHAPTER 27

It wasn't the first time that McCabe had experienced the phenomenon; seeing someone in an unfamiliar place, like a word out of context. But this was an extreme example.

Lieutenant Pat Kovarik was standing about three foot from him in the National Press Club.

Once he'd got over the surprise. McCabe's instinct was to laugh. He couldn't have been more surprised had a tiger walked into his local coffee shop and ordered a latte. There was more than one similarity in that comparison. He couldn't contain the laughter any longer; out it came.

'They'll take your badge away from you Kovarik, if any of your superiors catch sight of you in here.' The words were barely audible through the laughter. 'How did you know I was here?' Kovarik didn't look in any mood for laughter.

Not that the detective was known for his humour, but now his face was serious. He looked like a man on a mission. 'I just have to follow the empty bottles of whisky,' he said bluntly. The remark was his line in the sand. He wasn't playing games. 'Or in this case, the dead bodies.'

The smile disappeared from McCabe's face too.

Kovarik looked around, as another wave of members came into the lounge and moved towards the bar.

McCabe stood up. 'There's a room downstairs which I think we can use, unless it's booked for a press conference. I take it, by your look, you want to talk in private?'

A minute later they were seated opposite each other at the table in a small conference room, next to the club entrance.

'Isn't this cosy?' said McCabe trying to lower the tension. Kovarik still looked sombre but forced the semblance of a smile. He looked at his watch. 'I know you're a busy man,' he said sounding far from sincere. 'So I'll get to the point. I've two murders. You were in the vicinity of one.'

'I'm a suspect?' responded McCabe, trying to make light of the detective's comments.

'If I've to put up with your infantile humour, McCabe, we can go a few blocks down to police headquarters. The city is more than pleased to play host to people who think the police force are here for their amusement.'

McCabe knew he'd gone too far. He'd known the detective for several years. They were far from friends but he thought they had a respectful working relationship. It was a delicate balance which could easily be disturbed. On this occasion, he knew he'd crossed the line.

'Hang on. I wasn't making a joke about your work. Surely you know me well enough?'

Kovarik just stared at him for a moment. 'There's background to this story which I'm not privy to but I need to know.'

McCabe returned the detective's look. He really didn't think there was any possibility of sharing information. The detective

213

hated the Press and distrusted them even more. Not for the first time did they find themselves on the same road. He liked the detective who was dedicated and one of the good guys. But journalism and authority weren't supposed to mix.

McCabe was after the story. They both knew they had different agendas.

The fact that Kovarik was here suggested he was unhappy with his progress. When he was in such a frame of mind, caution was required.

'If I thought you were a suspect, you would have been locked up long before now.' The detective sounded as if he meant every word. 'That can still be accommodated.' He was laying his ground rules. It was obvious he wasn't playing games.

McCabe got the gist. There would be no friendly banter today.

'You went to see a Professor Draper, at Georgetown University, shortly before he was murdered.'

'I know.'

'You do?'

'Yes, Lieutenant, I do. I not only write news, I read it. It was on the front page of the *Washington Post*, among others.'

'Why were you there? I want to know the details,' he ordered, with the same serious tone.

It was McCabe's turn to outline his rules. 'You know how I operate and you know that there are confidences involved. We are both aware of the limitations. I'll help you if I can.'

'What does that mean?' asked Kovarik, sounding wary about agreeing to any conditions. 'This is a murder enquiry and whether you like it or not, you're involved.'

McCabe sensed he was back watching the delicate balance again. 'It's very simple, Lieutenant. A friend of mine died recently in Scotland. I went to his funeral and through that I'm on this story.' He shrugged his shoulders slightly but said nothing more. It was a vague answer. It was meant to be.

'That's it?' asked Kovarik with an edge to his voice. 'You went to a funeral and then what?' he added, showing his usual impatience.

McCabe shook his head, a little frustrated. He had the highest regard for the detective whose professional skills were exceptional and his tenacity admirable. But his impatience was more than irritating. 'The guy who died was a very close friend.' Kovarik's expression changed immediately. 'I'm sorry,' he said respectfully.

McCabe waved a hand in a dismissive gesture. 'He was a great journalist. I know you're not a great admirer of what we do but he was one of the best. He was an incessant digger. For him, getting a new story was almost like a fix. He was an addict, in that regard. He was on a story when he died.'

'So where does Draper come in?'

'I don't know but my friend had been at a conference in DC a few weeks ago, met Draper and had phoned him several times. So, I went to see him.' McCabe was uncomfortable to go any further but he knew the detective wouldn't be satisfied and

215

would keep pressing. He was confident that by now the detective would have found out about the senator too but possibly not his visit to the houseboat.

McCabe had gone as far as he was prepared to, at least for the moment. Perhaps it was time he asked some questions of his own? 'How come you showed up here anyway?'

'I told you, I followed the bodies,' he said. He chuckled, as he enjoyed his own joke.

'You went to the boat and someone told you I was here. Who was it?' asked McCabe, sounding annoyed.

Kovarik was enjoying himself. 'What is it you guys say? I can't disclose my sources.' He had another giggle. 'I also found out about your visitor, the senator.'

McCabe knew this police warhorse well. They were so much alike.

The detective was just as reticent about sharing his information too. He wouldn't even brief the Press unless it was in his interest. If he disclosed anything it was for a purpose. One never knew what was running through that clever analytical mind?

'I can't tell you anymore,' said McCabe firmly and stood up. 'You know the rules.'

'Can't or won't?' responded Kovarik, standing up too then walking towards the door. He turned as he got there. 'I have a few more questions but they can wait. Next time, I'll play host. You can come down to police headquarters and enjoy the hospitality of the city.'

Kovarik stopped in the doorway, as if he'd forgotten something.

'Then you can tell me all about Hanya Smolka.'

McCabe still had his mouth open when Kovarik walked out of the door.

CHAPTER 28

The presidential political fundraiser for a colleague of Senator Forsyth at the Hay-Adams historic hotel, a stone's throw from the White House, was getting tedious and the conversations repetitive. The senator never had any such lofty ambitions for his own career but often, particularly during these events, he'd wondered what might have happened had his life taken a different turn?

The smiles and the handshakes, which were expected and grew in number on each of these occasions, tested his mettle and drained him. At the end of every such marathon evening, despite the opulent setting and the luxury of the furnishings, he felt as if he'd had a workout at the local gym. He made one last effort, gave one final greeting to a generous donating tycoon, nodded to his chief of staff then made for the elevator.

His car arrived just as he reached the driveway at the front of the hotel. He could have had a driver but since he was going home, and it had been a hard day, he would enjoy the therapy of driving himself to Georgetown. It wouldn't be a long journey, barely twenty minutes, and then he could relax. His wife had gone to visit her mother, a joy he'd managed to avoid.

He tipped the valet and slid into the driver's seat. Lately he'd been thinking of getting a smaller car. A Lincoln Continental, while offering a level of luxury that he and his wife enjoyed, was a little too ostentatious and certainly unwieldy for the narrow streets of trendy Georgetown.

Half an hour later the car slid down the small pathway behind his house. The automatic garage doors opened and he carefully drove the car forward. He pressed the button on the remote control again and the garage door closed, almost silently, behind him. He pulled the keys out of the ignition then felt something cold and metallic push against the back of his right ear. The muzzle of a silencer rested just behind his earlobe. A voice from the darkness of the rear passenger seat explained the intrusion.

'Senator, get out of the car very slowly and keep your hands away from any pockets, where I can see them. I will be right behind you. We will be going into the house. Keep your eyes forward at all times.'

They walked slowly from the garage, up the small connecting stairwell into the house then through to the lounge, the gunman behind, steering his victim with the prod of his gun.

'The consignment; where is it?' said the gunman with another push of the barrel into the senator's neck.

'It has gone to Scotland,' answered the congressman in short gasps. He was having trouble breathing.

'We have more to talk about then,' said the intruder. 'I hope you have some answers.'

For the next several hours, the household lights in the senator's home switched on and off, as previously programmed. From the outside there was no sign of anything unusual. The postman had come and gone, as had the usual stream of dog walkers on their way to early morning jaunts in the local park. Even the small group of students who'd stopped to gossip as they walked to a morning lecture at the university about a half-dozen blocks away, didn't notice anything. There was no sign of any disturbance.

A half hour later the scene was totally different. The cleaner, arriving at the Forsyth house, had discovered the bloodied body on the lounge floor, phoned the police and an ambulance. Then the narrow cobblestoned road of the historic townhouse was a crime-scene and the traffic, students and tourists were diverted through the adjoining streets.

According to the local radio station, there had been an attempt on the life of a resident, Senator Dorman Forsyth. The good news was that the emergency services had reached him in time and he was on his way to the university's hospital, wired up to all the relevant mobile lifesaving equipment, with two medics monitoring his every move.

Kovarik had been alerted. He and John Henry were on their way and arrived at the hospital minutes after Forsyth. The emergency medical treatment prevented them getting anywhere near the victim. The progress of the medics could only be gauged from a distance, through one glass window of the emergency room. That was limited too. Most of the vision was obscured by some piece of equipment or ancillary tubes and wires.

Predictably, Kovarik paced outside the room while John Henry sat quietly watching the doctors and nurses come and go. Occasionally he would catch the eye of a medic in transit. So far, all he received was a shake of the head. It was clear that Forsyth was in a bad way. They had no idea what had happened. The information was scant.

It was two hours before they had any useful dialogue with a doctor, a surgeon who'd just completed an operation on the victim. 'He's traumatized; a serious head wound, the result of a vicious assault.'

The Lieutenant lost no time. He was in the surgeon's face in seconds. 'Did he say anything?'

The doctor stepped back, a little surprised by the detective's approach.

Kovarik realized his error. 'I am sorry, doctor. But it's vital that we get some clue as to what happened. We believe it's connected to another attack.'

John Henry looked at the detective strangely. A link between this assault and any other was news to him.

Kovarik sensed his unease and nodded to him. 'Yes, we believe there is a connection between this assault and another. Can you tell me anything?' he continued pressing the doctor.

The doctor looked a little more relaxed. 'Judging by the beating, it suggests a frenzied attack which was meant to kill. But it is a little unusual.'

'In what regard,' fired Kovarik instantly.

The doctor hesitated slightly. 'This is only speculative but the wounds suggest to me that there was a beating over a fairly sustained period.'

'Persuasion?' asked Kovarik.

The doctor looked puzzled.

'It could be some thuggish ritual but more likely the attacker was after something,' added John Henry. 'As the Lieutenant said, perhaps a barbaric method of persuasion.'

'When can we speak to him?' asked the detective.

'That might be some time off, Lieutenant.'

Kovarik looked restless. 'Is he unconscious?'

The surgeon nodded. 'Yes he is but he should come around in a few hours. However, that is only one issue.'

'Simply put, in layman's terms, the lower part of his right jaw is broken. He may have trouble talking with any coherence until we can repair the damage.'

'How long?' pressed Kovarik again.

'Lieutenant, these things can't be rushed. We'll need to take this a day at a time.'

Kovarik didn't say a word on the elevator ride to the main hospital entrance. He was unhappy with the medical prognosis.

John Henry was still waiting for an explanation, as they crossed the parking lot.

The Lieutenant clicked the car doors open. 'You looked surprised when I mentioned that there had been another assault.'

'I wasn't surprised at that, it was the inference there was a connection.'

'There is,' shouted Kovarik. 'I know there is.' He was loud and soon realized it. He checked round about to make sure he hadn't attracted attention. 'Sorry,' he said quietly, as he eased into the driver's seat. 'You know I don't believe in coincidences.'

John Henry thought for a moment. He needed to choose his words carefully, particularly if Kovarik was so incensed. 'Sir, because it can't be accepted as a coincidence, it doesn't mean there is a connection.'

The detective said nothing, started the car and drove the short distance to the senator's house. 'Then we'll just have to prove there is a connection. Get forensic here to go through the house with their finest touch. Also get some manpower and have them knock on every door in the street. Whoever did this is not invisible.'

John Henry was well aware of the Kovarik methodology and philosophy. A crime can't be committed, nor assailants come and go without a trace being left. It might be faint, he would maintain, but it must be there and it was their job to find it.

Three hours later, even with the assistance of forensic science, they had nothing of any consequence. They'd taken fingerprints but whether any were of use and could be compared with any on file, was a wild shot.

The half dozen uniforms they'd managed to acquire did an excellent job, doggedly going from house to house and a few commercial premises, in the hope of bagging a witness. Surely you couldn't beat a man to within an inch of his life without making a noise or attracting some attention?

There was now a wad of statements for John Henry's consumption. Invariably they were dotted with contradictions. The man they had seen was tall, others claimed medium. He was fair, others insisted he was dark. He was in his twenties but a few were adamant he was middle-aged. He felt they were asking the wrong questions to the wrong people.

Forensic did come up with one clue; the main door to the house was locked. There was every indication that the door was rarely used. It could mean that the senator usually entered his house via the garage. Perhaps the assailant was waiting for him in the garage, although there was no indication of forced entry there either. That left only one possibility; the attacker was already in the car when the congressman left for home.

John Henry was on his phone in seconds. 'I'm glad I caught you,' he said apologetically.

'Not another long shot,' was the reply from the forensic lab.

John Henry winced. Of course it was. That's what their job was all about; chase the possibilities and eliminate them one by one. 'Probably,' he said quietly. 'But I know you guys do such a great job when I ask you,' he added, delivering the compliment with his characteristic charm.

'OK, John Henry, let's have it. I was hoping to get home for the ball game.'

'I want you to check the car. It's a hunch too.'

'We did and the garage too. There was nothing but a few prints. We got nothing from them either.'

John Henry's face fell. 'Damn!' he whispered.

'The garage is operated by a remote in the car but it can be opened manually from inside too; a safety feature I guess. That's the way he left, we reckoned,' said the forensic.

'So he'd have to walk down that alleyway to get out?' asked John Henry.

'Yes, just by the sandwich shop on the corner of the main drag, if my memory serves me right.'

John Henry quickly checked the statements again. There was nothing from anyone in the sandwich shop. 'OK, I'll check it myself in the morning. Thanks.'

It was barely 6 am when John Henry pulled up outside the shop at the bottom of the lane. Trade was brisk. He sat in the car watching, observing an entire new world; students with their books, tradesman carrying tools and even clergy in full cassock. It was breakfast time. He was in the mood now himself. A large cup of coffee and a bagel would go down well. According to the sign above *Good Bite,* it was open until one o'clock in the morning. He flipped through the file containing the statements which rested on the passenger seat; definitely no mention of the shop.

He gave his order at the counter, watching the waves of human traffic come and go. Surely someone would have seen something? The man on the cash register seemed to be the boss, most of the other staffers looked like students. He paid his check then showed his badge. 'Were you around yesterday?'

The cashier gave him a strange look. 'I'm here all the time. I literally live above the shop.' He laughed.

John Henry gave him a sympathetic smile.

'But we were closed most of the day; boiler repairs.'

'Our team was checking the neighbourhood yesterday in case.....'

'Yes, the senator,' the cashier interrupted. 'I heard; terrible. It's barely a block away but we never hear anything. It's quiet round here after midnight.'

'But you were closed?'

'We were still open early morning yesterday. Then we were closed. But, as I told you, I live here. I was in and out until late with garbage. There's always something to do here.'

'Did you see anyone?' asked John Henry.

'It's a quiet neighbourhood at that time but if there's someone about you notice them.'

'Did you see anyone come down the alleyway early yesterday morning?'

The cashier seemed hesitant. 'I was tired. I didn't get a clear view. It was dark. But I did see someone.'

John Henry thought for a moment. He could hear Kovarik's prediction in his ear. The detective's instincts were usually good. They were worth examining.

He pulled out his cell phone, pressed a few buttons and showed the shopkeeper the picture on the screen. 'Would you have seen this man,' he asked, flashing the photo of Solokov.

'I did see a figure come down the lane but no more,' said the cashier, shaking his head.

'What time?'

The man thought for a moment, began to say something then stopped. 'I'd just closed up and was putting out the garbage. I'd say about 1.30.'

'And you don't think it was this guy?' asked John Henry, showing him the photo again.

'I didn't say it wasn't him,' he said, hesitating again. 'I said, I couldn't recognise him from the photo. It's not the clearest photo.'

John Henry smiled. 'Sorry, it's the best we have.'

'This guy is a suspect then?'

It was a good question. John Henry didn't have an answer. He was definitely grasping at straws. They had three possible suspects for the Georgetown murder; one was a woman, the two others were men but one was dead. If Kovarik's instincts were right and he had a damn good track record then Solokov was a good bet. 'We're just exploring options, that's all; eliminating possibilities.'

'He was a big guy, I'd say about 6.3 and bald. Yes, I saw his head flash in the street lamp,' he said moving closer to John Henry and peering at the photo again. 'Difficult to say but I guess it could be him.'

CHAPTER 29

On his houseboat, McCabe had just listened to a CNN report on the senator's attack. He flicked from one TV channel to another in search of more information. As usual, the networks didn't know much and, as was now commonplace, they speculated. The vast appetite of 24-hour news required it to be filled with something. Dead air was the only sin. At all costs fill the slots.

Today, there was no shortage of guesswork. Theories abounded from a terrorist attack to a heart condition due to a heavy workload. The senator had been alone in his Georgetown house when the incident occurred. His body, so the reports determined, had been found by his cleaner.

McCabe wasn't happy with any of the broadcasts. None made any sense. There was no report of foul play. Nobody made any link with the death of the Georgetown Physics Professor, barely days before.

The professor was dead and the senator had been seriously injured, whatever the motive. There had to be a connection. What little he did know began to disturb him. Those two victims were directly connected with the story that Gallagher had been following when he died in the car accident. It was claimed that there was no evidence that the car had been tampered with but it was certainly true that he had been working on an important story which involved Draper and Forsyth. He now could see some of the pieces fitting together.

At first sight neither of these parties had anything in common. However, the senator's work was steeped in the shadowland of national security. In that world, nothing was what it appeared to be. It begged the question; what interest did Draper and his friend Gallagher have with these professional illusionists? The British security presence at the Scottish funeral would seem to confirm the connection..

And what of the Russians? While he would have liked to have thought that Hanya's interest in him was entirely personal, he knew otherwise. Many years ago during the cold war, she'd been trusted enough to rub shoulders with the western Press when the political climate was far more certain. She was an even safer pair of hands now, trusted implicitly by those who wielded power in the KGB. He enjoyed her company immensely, and would continue to do so, but she'd appeared in his life out of the blue, for a purpose yet to be disclosed. Her paymasters appeared to be interested in Gallagher's story too. By definition, they could be involved in the murder of the Georgetown professor and, what looked like, the attempted murder of Senator Forsyth?

Then, of course, there was Dounreay. In the UK it meant atomic power and all the political nuances that went with it. The name had obviously some clout in the US too. The very mention of it was enough for the senator to make a premature and sudden exit.

McCabe looked at his watch. He was meeting Hanya. Perhaps he'd get some answers to those questions. He would also like to know why Kovarik, of the DC Homicide Police, was interested in her? The detective's parting line had been thrown at him for dramatic effect. The clever and tenacious Kovarik did nothing without purpose.

Benvenuti was a small, family-owned, intimate Italian Restaurant, just north of Dupont Circle in North West Washington. The lamb, the liver and the pasta dishes were legendary. So were the people who, supposedly, had eaten there over the decades. Members of Congress and Presidents had graced its tables as had others with more notoriety.

Among the celebrities, whose pictures hung on the walls, were movie stars and gangsters, the latter who no doubt visited while they were giving evidence to a nervous Congress. They all added to the mystique of the place.

McCabe was seated opposite Hanya, who looked even more breathtaking than normal. How could he possibly ask her the questions he'd been rehearsing during the past half hour? As before, she ordered a vodka martini and he a large scotch. He'd leave the questions until later. They scoured the menu. He recommended one dish then another. In the end, she settled for the lamb shank cooked in red wine and he the calf's liver cooked in butter and sage. Two excellent bottles of Chianti completed the culinary ecstasy. They skipped the dessert and went straight to the brandies.

He felt in a far more relaxed mood now. He was hoping she was too. There was no other way to tackle the issue but head-on.

'Why is Lieutenant Kovarik, of DC Homicide, interested in you?' he asked. It wasn't entirely true but it would provoke some response, he hoped.

She continued to sip her brandy for a moment. 'I didn't realise he was?'

'Let me make the question general, then?'

'Why are the police interested in you?'

 He wasn't sure how far he could push her, even after such a splendid dinner, and the after-effects of good wine and brandy. But he was going to try. He was still hoping she'd come along just to enjoy his company but his instinct told him otherwise. She was here to either steer him towards a goal or be with him when he got there. That could only mean they were after the same thing. But he still wasn't sure what that could be.

'I wanted to talk to the professor who was murdered. I went to his office but he wasn't there. His body was discovered the following morning. I saw no body, dead or otherwise. I told the police that.'

McCabe looked a little surprised. 'Why were you there?' he asked, half knowing the answer. It was now obvious. He was certain. She was following the same trail as him.

'I needed some information.' Her answer told him nothing.

 He finished his brandy and called the waiter for another two. He leaned over the table towards her. 'Hanya, I know you've a job to do and I'm enjoying you doing it. But what's this all about?'

'Is this when we fall into each other's arms and confess all?' She laughed out loud.

231

He still wasn't sure if she was playing games. Telling her all he knew in an exchange for her information was a risky strategy which still required a degree of trust. Not a decision to be made in the wake of a good dinner, he thought. Would he be full of regrets when he sobered up? 'I'm going to finish a story which, as you know, an old friend of mine started. I owe it to him.'

'Is that it? Not much of an exchange, is it?'

The brandies arrived. He took one and passed the other across to her. 'The rest is vague but I know they're connected. How, I'm not sure.'

'What's the story?'

He took another swig. 'Don't push me on this. Let me do it at my own pace.'

She took a sip from her new glass while watching him.

'It involves Dounreay; I'm sure you're aware what that once represented?'

She nodded.

'It's not at the forefront of development now. It is being decommissioned but used as a dumping ground for unwanted nuclear waste.'

'The Americans were supposed to deliver a consignment there which they took from Georgia,' she commented.

'I thought they did?' he asked, looking puzzled.

'Supposedly; the Russians asked for confirmation about its destination but the Americans didn't provide it, or wouldn't, or couldn't.'

'Why would the Russians want that?'

She took another sip of brandy. 'Our business is full of rumour and counter-rumour. But it is believed the Americans took it as bait for a terrorist group. The Russians would never have agreed to that.'

'What's in Dounreay then?' McCabe asked.

She shrugged her shoulders.

'You thought the professor might know?'

She nodded. 'He monitored the movement of nuclear waste around the globe. He compiles data on those movements. He is, or was, the living authority. We thought that Andy Gallagher with the help of the murdered Georgetown professor was writing a story about the Georgia consignment. Draper had written many academic papers speculating on missing nuclear waste. Then you turned up. We thought it a Godsend.'

'I thought you guys didn't believe in God,' he said, trying to lighten the atmosphere. 'Is that why they drafted you in because we had known each other before? So you could stay close to the story?' he added.

She didn't smile. 'It's too serious for games. If the Americans don't or won't confirm where this consignment has gone, the Russians will think the worst; back to the cold war and their relationship of mutual distrust. And then where do we go?'

He dropped any attempt at humour. 'And the senator; everybody thought he might have an inside track? Is that why he is involved?'

She nodded again. 'Certainly we thought he would be the best informed. But again it was speculation. No one knew anything.'

'Are the Russians responsible for the attacks?' asked McCabe bluntly.

She hesitated. 'Yes and no. I can't tell you the details. It's too.....' She stopped in mid-sentence. 'But it's something that needs to be dealt with, immediately; something needs to be done.'

Hanya Smolka parked her car discreetly at the far end of the parking lot away from the main entrance to George Washington University Hospital. She walked to the reception area quickly. The fragrant smell from the huge bunch of flowers she carried was quite pronounced.

She'd been told the room that the senator was occupying. The elevator was crowded with visitors, medics and trolleys. She took it all the way to the top floor, waited until the elevator was ready to return then pressed the button for the floor below. She was gambling the carriage would be empty on the way down. If not she would wait again; she was in no hurry.

The attack on the senator had appalled her. The photo which the young policeman had shown her on his cellphone shocked her even more. She had dealt with the man in the photo before; a ruthless sadistic, psychopath. Where had he come from and was that one of Krupin's manic ideas. Even he should surely realize that the crude methodology of Solokov, in which assassinations and beatings were commonplace, was not a strategy to be countenanced in Washington, where confrontations were subtle and the weapons diplomatic.

She had no doubt in her mind. The attacks on the Georgetown professor and the senator were hallmarks of Solokov's style. Such violence sat comfortably with him who, as an ex KGB operator, had a license to employ any method he so wished to secure his goals.

What role was Krupin now playing? She was uncertain. Perhaps she did Krupin an injustice and this strategy was not of his making but it had been forced on him by Moscow? Whoever was responsible had got it wrong, very wrong. Solokov's end-game was crass, he had little foresight or imagination and was an ill-fit for Washington.

There were few details released in the Press about the senator or his welfare. Perhaps, without being too obvious, she could find out what had happened and how serious was the mess Solokov had made? That's why she was here.

By luck, her elevator strategy proved right. She was the only one travelling down from the top floor. It was an attempt, feeble or otherwise, to minimise the number who may witness or notice her visit. Again she was lucky. When the doors opened she slipped out into an empty corridor. There were two uniformed patrolmen, stationed at the far end of the hallway, on either side of one of the rooms. She read the room number on the door nearest and counted down towards the policemen. If she was right, they were guarding the senator. There was little point now in going any further.

She turned round quickly and almost collided with a young doctor. She was caught by surprise. 'These are for Senator Forsyth,' she stammered, before she'd given it any thought.

The young doctor smiled as he looked at her, as enchanted by her as he was with the flowers. 'I'm sure you would like to deliver them yourself,' he said looking down towards the room guarded by the patrolmen. Both policemen looked in his direction.

Instantly she realised she had a problem when one of the uniforms began walking towards her. She thrust the flowers into the doctors arms then smiled at him with all her charm. 'I'm only here to deliver them,' she said turning quickly and making for the elevator. She took the stairs instead and disappeared, leaving the young doctor, surprised and disappointed, holding the bouquet.

Two flights of stairs down, she took the elevator to the ground level. It had been a risky strategy. She'd learned something; the police were now taking no chances. As she'd suspected, Solokov's mindless antics had taken this issue to a whole new level.

CHAPTER 30

There had been a sudden and unexpected turn of events. John Henry found himself hurrying, after he got a brief and blunt phone call from Kovarik. The address was two blocks from the Russian embassy. He had no details other than a body had been discovered by an early morning jogger. The bloodied corpse left little doubt that the person had been shot. That was one stark observation that needed no forensic confirmation.

Kovarik stood at the head of a body. He inspected what could be seen of the face then walked round the body, slumped to one side. He peered at what looked like a gunshot wound in the neck. It wasn't a huge hole but clearly it had done the job. Was it the work of a marksman or just a lucky shot? One thing was certain. It was a handgun wound, so the killer must have been close.

John Henry's car pulled up behind a patrol car. Paramedics from an ambulance were kneeling beside what he assumed was the victim. He got out of the car carefully and stood at the other side of the corpse to Kovarik.

The detective was still drinking his coffee as he walked round the body, surveying the immediate surroundings. He bent down, looked at the wound and followed the line of the shot over the sidewalk to the other side of the road. He stood up and inspected the small brick garden wall behind, running parallel to the sidewalk and the corpse. He bent down and pointed to a hole in the brickwork. He called over to John Henry. 'Look at that,' he said, moving closer and peering at the tiny hollow. 'I said look at it,' he shouted impatiently.

John Henry jumped forward and did as he was told. It was very small. Only a trained eye would have spotted it at all. He had to admit that he would have missed it. But it was a distinct cavity.

'What do you think that is?' The Lieutenant was carefully easing something from the hole.

Before John Henry could answer, a bullet popped out of the wall and fell onto the sidewalk.

'There's your answer,' said Kovarik, picking it up carefully and dropping it into an envelope. 'But no gun on the body,' he observed.

'What do you think?' he asked looking directly at the young policeman.

'Presumably it wasn't fired after the man had been shot, so it happened before,' he said confidently.

Kovarik nodded. 'So the gunman had at least two shots, assuming there is only one in the body. Perhaps he just sprayed the victim?'

'With two shots?'

Kovarik stood still, thinking. He shook his head. It would appear he didn't like the explanation. He moved towards John Henry and handed him the envelope. 'Get forensic,' he began to say and stopped. The young policeman appeared distracted.

John Henry was staring at the corpse. He bent down and studied the face. It wasn't easy to get a clear impression, since blood obscured part of it and some had begun to cake on the skin. He stood up and looked up at Kovarik, pulled his cellphone from his coat, fiddled with a few controls then looked at the screen. He bent down again with the phone image beside the victim's face. 'There's no doubt, Lieutenant. It's our man from the campus video, the one we thought might have killed the professor and possibly attacked the senator; definitely. He clicked the phone again and brought up another file. 'Colonel Nikita Solokov, supposedly a trade attaché at the Russian Embassy.'

'Damn,' said Kovarik under his breath. 'We're in the shit now.'

Kovarik loved Washington. He'd moved several years before from Baltimore, Maryland and never regretted the change. There were some things he missed about the old waterfront town but on the whole he was happy with the move.

But he constantly found himself with problems when dealing with the political manipulations of Washington. It was a hotbed of politics. That much was a given but it was much more. It was a breeding ground for every devious manoeuvre known to those, whose appetite for power and influence knew no bounds. Not for the first time had he been cautioned by his superiors to tread carefully when entering the delicate world of international diplomacy. Incidents could be provoked by a simple unforeseen incident, he was warned, so extra care was needed. He knew that to ignore such warnings could be costly. But he found it difficult to accept the restrictions. Anything which prevented him doing his job, he couldn't take in his stride. He admitted it was a deficiency and he'd be a better candidate for promotion if he could comply. He couldn't. Now he sensed he was heading for another such crisis, if he wasn't careful.

Two phone-enquires later and they were steered to the office of Andrei Krupin. His job description, at the Russian Embassy, seemed to embrace everything from trade to external affairs.

Kovarik had the feeling that the Russian was the primary gatekeeper. He sensed his patience was about to be tested once more.

John Henry sat beside the Lieutenant in Krupin's outer office on the second floor of the Russian Embassy.

Kovarik couldn't sit for long. He walked to the window and looked at the gardens which seemed to calm him a little. However, before long, he was looking at his watch and pacing up and down again.

Fortunately, within minutes, they were called into the Russian's office. John Henry was more than relieved.

Krupin, a stocky man with obvious Slavic features, jumped to his feet and greeted them with very vigorous handshakes.

Kovarik seemed surprised by the reception.

John Henry suspected the cordiality wouldn't last long.

'Please, do sit down,' said Krupin directing them to chairs in front of his desk. 'I wasn't sure how I could assist you. Of a confidential nature, you said. Because of our status, we rarely have direct contact with the police,' he said leaning back in his large leather chair.

'Your status?' repeated Kovarik completely deadpan.

'Our diplomatic status,' replied Krupin with a broad smile.

The DC diplomatic community, although most were competitors rather than members of a fraternity, promoted their respective country's agenda to those in Congress and the White House who would listen. In theory, they were also immune from prosecution; a privilege enjoyed through America's largesse, supposedly an international protocol, but which Kovarik abhorred and tested on every given occasion.

John Henry knew from the Russian's tone, it was only a matter of time before the atmosphere would turn rancid. Kovarik wouldn't be spoken to in such a fashion; as if he was a bell-hop and the Russian was doing him a favour.

John Henry cringed and waited for the onslaught.

'This is not a social call,' Kovarik said bluntly. 'It's about a member of your staff or delegation, whatever you call it here,' he said dismissively. 'He was found dead this morning, only a few blocks from here.'

'Dead?' asked Krupin.

John Henry thought the reaction strange. There was no alarm in the Russian's voice. Perhaps that was his style. Or maybe he knew already.

'Murdered; shot,' continued Kovarik.

John Henry pulled out his notebook and found the appropriate page. 'Nikita Solokov,' he said, making an obvious effort to get the pronunciation correct.

Krupin moved forward in his chair, took out a cigarette, offered the pack to them then lit it without apology. 'One of the privileges of working here,' he joked. 'The ban on smoking in

241

public places doesn't affect us on Russian soil,' he added, almost arrogantly.

Kovarik, a struggling ex-smoker, winced and looked far from impressed. He was trying to keep his inner passions under control. His reputedly short fuse was burning fast towards an inevitable end.

'Nikita Solokov,' repeated Krupin. 'Can't say I recognise the name, Lieutenant.'

John Henry felt the silence was deafening.

Kovarik looked as if he was about to explode.

John Henry intervened immediately, before the Lieutenant had a chance to respond. He respected the detective and loved the passion the Lieutenant displayed in circumstances like these. However, John Henry felt he could be more measured, more in control and certainly less impetuous.

He read from his notebook again. 'He arrived from Moscow a few days ago at Dulles Airport, as a member of the trade delegation here under a diplomatic passport, we have been informed. His name is actually Colonel Nikita Solokov, one time a member of the Russian security agency.'

Krupin, again showed no obvious emotion, although the result of his nervous chain-smoking was filling up the ashtray. He turned to the computer on his desk and typed in a few instructions. The screen filled with a listing. 'Yes, of course, I know who you mean now. I haven't had the pleasure of meeting with him yet,' he said unconvincingly.

John Henry could see Kovarik was ready to boil over. The Lieutenant could detect a lie even if he was wearing ear-mufflers. He had Krupin down as a liar. However, this time, it was too late to intervene.

'Solokov,' fired Kovarik, intentionally omitting the title.

'Solokov, whom you claim not to have met, was a suspect in two murders and also in an attempted murder,' he said slowly, staring straight at the Russian.

Krupin inhaled his cigarette heavily. 'Really!'

'Would you know why he was visiting a Professor Draper, a physicist at Georgetown University or Senator Dorman Forsyth, at his home, also in Georgetown?' Kovarik asked.

Krupin continued to smoke incessantly. He shrugged his shoulders. 'I'm afraid I can't help you there,' he said from behind the billows of a thick tobacco cloud.

The Lieutenant was still pushing. He wasn't leaving with nothing. 'We believe that Solokov had a gun with him but there was nothing found on his body.'

'I'm sorry, I wouldn't know, Lieutenant. We don't issue firearms to staff. What people do privately is their own business.'

Kovarik didn't believe a word of it. He was still pushing. 'If he was involved, I wouldn't be too confident that he would be immune from prosecution,' insisted the detective. He knew it was a dubious claim but he delivered the line nevertheless.

Krupin stubbed a half-smoked cigarette into the ashtray, which by now was almost full of butts, then stood up. 'Can I assume that his body will be brought here, Lieutenant? We have certain formalities. And of course we will be responsible for its repatriation.'

Kovarik knew he should have asked for permission to authorise an autopsy. He wasn't going to tell Krupin his plans. 'Of course, our people will notify you.'

'Thank you for informing me. I'm sorry I can't be more helpful,' said the Russian, as he pressed a button on his desk.

An athletic looking man opened the office door and stood to attention in silence.

The policemen left.

John Henry could tell, the Lieutenant was not happy.

CHAPTER 31

The forensic lab always smelled of formaldehyde. It irritated Kovarik beyond measure.

The head of the forensic team emerged, dressed in his customary green outfit, with a cup of coffee in his hand. He looked as if he was relaxing on his patio. 'Would you like a cup, Lieutenant. It'll help you forget the surroundings.' He smiled amicably, sensing the detective's discomfort. He didn't wait for an answer but walked to the percolator beside the wall and poured another cup.

Kovarik looked at his watch. 'Can we get straight to your report doctor?'

The forensic was quickly back by Kovarik's side and handed him the cup. 'Relax, Lieutenant, our man is not going anywhere,' he said, nodding to the body on the slab.

He knew the detective never liked the lab environment but he sensed that today there was something else nagging him. It didn't take much insight into human nature to know that Kovarik was from the old school where they believed in traditional police methods and hated having to rely on science to prove a case. He'd heard stories from junior policemen that the detective drilled them in his methodology and insisted they do not rely on forensic. Kovarik was one of those who thought his profession was now being held hostage to science.

'I'm never sure, Lieutenant, if you feel we are an intrusion into police work, or if you find our contribution worthwhile.'

Kovarik looked slightly awkward. He made no secret of his dislike of the policemen who were incompetent or lazy and left it to science to prove a case. 'I have no doubt of the value of modern methods,' he said, sounding vague and non-committal. 'But it doesn't replace good police-work'.

The forensic smiled. He knew how professional Kovarik was and how that ethos was instilled in everyone who worked with him. The detective's caustic and abrasive style was difficult to stomach sometimes but he never doubted his ability or commitment. 'OK, let's do it,' he said as he pulled away the sheet covering the body of Solokov.

'There's nothing much to add to the observations you've already made at the crime scene. And correct observations they were too. I read your report with interest.' He walked to a small desk at his side, picked up a folder, turned a few pages then stopped. 'Your diagram of the shooting angle is quite accurate, remarkably so,' he said closing the folder. 'You drew it from the position of the bullet in the wall.' He stopped and looked at Kovarik who was studying the naked body on the slab. 'Did you follow what I was saying, Lieutenant?'

It was meant to be a compliment but Kovarik didn't react. The detective finished inspecting the body but now seemed deep in thought. It looked as if something had just occurred to him. 'Was the angle of the bullet in the wall the same?'

Forensic smiled. This detective was no amateur. 'Compared with the bullet in the body?'

Kovarik look at him. 'That's what I mean,' he added and turned to point to the wound in the body.

'They are different,' said the forensic. 'You've a good eye, detective, maybe you should have been a forensic specialist.'

Kovarik grinned.

It wasn't clear to the scientist whether the policeman found the remark amusing. He liked to think so. 'You're wondering how the bullets could come from two different directions?' he added.

'I thought about that before I examined the body detail. It is a bit strange.'

'Well?' asked Kovarik, trying to anticipate the conclusion. He looked a little puzzled.

'Simple,' said forensic. 'They came from different directions because they were fired by two gunmen. '

'What?'

'The bullet in the wall, which you gave me, DID NOT come from the same gun as the one in the body,' said the forensic with emphasis.

Kovarik looked even more puzzled. He was trying to analyse the information and understand its implications.

'Your police-work could only go so far. And you did damn well. You have observational skills second to no one I've ever worked with,' said the forensic, complimenting Kovarik again. The detective was still deep in thought and barely nodded an acknowledgement. He was still obviously confused.

'Lieutenant, the bullets were different, the direction in which they were fired was different, the places they were fired from were different and, by definition, so were the gunmen.'

'But how could that be?' asked Kovarik.

The scientist had anticipated the question. 'The shots had to be fired within seconds of each other, the shot on the wall being first then the one in the body next. The victim was turning towards the angle of the first shot when the second one struck him.'

Kovarik walked to the desk and picked up the folder with his sketch of the shooting. 'Two gunmen,' he said, as he studied the diagram.

The forensic joined the detective at the desk, took the folder and turned to another page. 'Here is my drawing of the shooting,' he said pushing it towards Kovarik.

The detective studied the sketch in silence. 'What's your take on it then?'

The forensic was always hesitant to give too much analysis. Kovarik could be touchy about such speculation. 'It's only guesswork, Lieutenant. I know you like the detection to be left to the police. But there is a case to be considered where the gunmen didn't know about each other and still don't.'

'Why?'

'The ballistics on the bullets suggests that silencers were used on both guns. The shot to the body was very lucky or was the shot of a marksman. Whoever he was, he knew he only needed one shot. Let's suppose that was the case and, a split second before,

248

another less competent gunman had discharged a shot but then saw him fall.'

'That's incredible.'

'Yes but perfectly possible. The scientific facts support it.'

Kovarik was somewhere else in his thoughts again. 'And they wouldn't know about each other?'

'Each one thinking he'd killed the Solokov.'

Kovarik murmured what sounded like a thanks as he made towards the door, still deep in thought.

CHAPTER 32

There were bells from an unrecognisable church tower. McCabe could see a handbell being rung in a school yard. The images were a muddle but the sound was far away and then it was near. He woke with a start and realised he'd been dreaming. His cell phone was ringing and it danced about the small drawer-set by his bedside. The time was displayed prominently on its front. It was only six o'clock.

'While you've been sleeping, McCabe, the world has moved on.' Stan Walker sniggered at the other end of the phone. 'It's pissing down here. Why should you not share in our misery?' He giggled again.

'The world's on different time clocks too. It's six o'clock in the bloody morning.'

'I know but I'm on a promise later, so this was the only slot.'

McCabe, still trying to waken up, could guess what the event was which Walker had so delicately described as *a promise*. Knowing his friend and his insatiable appetite for the sexually challenging, he'd guess that a neighbour's wife would be entertained while her husband was on the golf course. 'Is this a new challenge or a recycled one?' He shouldn't really have asked but he couldn't resist.

'If I thought you were interested, I would elaborate but I know you don't care and I don't have time.'

McCabe laughed quietly. 'OK. What have you got?'

'There are a couple of things which might be of interest.'

McCabe could hear the rustle of paper at the end of the phone.

'I took that listing you sent me to a numbers' contact of mine.'

'*Numbers*?'

'That's the nickname I give him. He's a statistician but he also likes to play the horses.'

Another flawed contact of Walker, thought McCabe.

'I know what you're thinking but he knows his stuff.'

'Did he get fired too; for cooking the books?'

Walker sighed. The sound of his frustration was fairly audible.

'I don't know why you're so fucking hung up about where the information comes from. You don't have any problems using it.'

McCabe had the utmost confidence in Walker and the quality of his information. But he did like a tease. 'OK, pal, you have my full attention.'

Walker smiled in satisfaction and began reading down the listing. 'According to him, it's a delivery schedule'.

'What kind of delivery schedule?'

'Just hang on. Let me read what he's written on the paper you sent me.' There was silence for a moment. 'He thinks one column of numbers is a weight, the second is a delivery date and the third he didn't know.'

'Did you tell him the context?' asked McCabe. He was hoping they might throw a light on what story Gallagher was chasing.

'Someone broke into my houseboat. They could have been after it. I couldn't make out what it was, so I thought you might.'

'It sure as hell wasn't a list of your sexual exploits,' replied Walker with a loud laugh. It was his turn for the banter. He couldn't resist.

'OK. I think I've heard that infantile joke before. Do you think we can move on?' McCabe sounded a little irritated.

'A few items, which I hope, might be of interest to you.' Walker stopped talking for a moment. 'You know, a thought has occurred to me. This might be the link you were looking for.'

'Stan what are you talking about?' McCabe by this time had slipped on a robe, made his way to the galley and was making a pot of coffee.

'The senator you went to see...'

'Someone attacked him in his home,' interrupted McCabe.

'It was in the news here too.'

'They're trying to play it down but it's difficult, given who he is. The police won't say anything.'

'That doesn't stop the speculation; it makes it worse,' commented Walker.

McCabe poured himself a cup of coffee, took it and sat down on the sofa. He felt he'd been up for ages. 'Well, what was the great thought?'

'Dorman Forsyth made a very interesting speech a few months ago in the senate. I'll have to refer to the transcript. I can send you a copy or give you the reference. The essence is that US National Security is his bag and he was insisting that uranium fuel be flown out of Soviet Georgia, to prevent it falling into the hands of terrorists. He was demanding that it be done as a matter

252

of urgency. Was that the Dounreay consignment you asked me to check?'

'Yes, it was,' said McCabe very slowly.

'Well, I checked with my security contacts here. They said, at the time, the Russians went along with the idea of the Americans taking a consignment of nuclear waste out of Georgia. But things have got a bit tense since. I gather they wanted the Americans to confirm everything had gone to plan. That was part of the senator's plan too.'

'And?'

Walker raised his eyebrows and shrugged. 'And he's the guy someone tried to kill?'

McCabe walked to his desk and fired up his laptop. A patchwork of his regular newsfeeds came up on the screen. He made a few quick checks. 'No obvious progress report on the senator. He is still with us.'

'I'll let you know if anything else turns up at this end,' added Walker. He sounded confused too.

'Send me through that transcript and anything else you've got. I think there could be a link there,' said McCabe, as he hung up. He clicked on the different elements of his screen mosaic but there was no update on the congressman.

Since it was Kovarik in charge, the information would be tightly controlled. The detective believed that the police held the advantage if only they had access to detailed crime information. Anyone on his team who ever contemplated leaking to the Press wouldn't be in a job for long.

253

An email alert flashed across McCabe's computer screen. He hit the acceptance key. The screen filled with text from Walker.

According to the Congressman, he was concerned about five kilograms of enriched Uranium, contained in reactor fuel assemblies housed at the research centre in the former Soviet Republic of Georgia.

He said in his speech. 'The US needs to commit to taking custody of this fuel and transport it safely from the Physics Research Institute at Mtskheta, about ten miles from Tbilisi, the Georgian capital. The US should be worried that such a deadly payload could fall into the hands of Chechen terrorists or Iran. It is vital that this enriched Uranium, which is tailor-made for nuclear weapons, be properly and securely protected.'

He also quoted a Professor Draper's academic paper about the dangers of poor security in complexes housing nuclear fuel and specifically referenced Georgia.

My sources tell me the Americans flew the Soviet payload to Dounreay. That's why the Brits had an active interest. The operation was supposed to be secret but then, for some inexplicable reason, it became very public. But, as I've told you before, there was also a report that the consignment was flawed and what arrived in Scotland was not what left Georgia. That would also account for any Russian paranoia.

Good luck in sorting that mess out.

Yet again, this information linked the professor and the senator. It was classic news-fodder for Andy Gallagher too. Now Senator Dorman Forsyth was the only one left alive. He was the one with the answers.

If McCabe had been in any doubt, he wasn't now. He needed to speak to the senator.

CHAPTER 33

McCabe was never comfortable with any arrangement with the police which required him to disclose information. He was supposed to be a member of the Fourth Estate and the police were part of the authoritative power that needed to be challenged. He must have said and written it a million times.

That was the theory and he'd lectured at many a university journalism school, preaching the same to enthusiastic wannabes. But the real world was different where the art of compromise was as prevalent as any other practice. Ethics aside, the strategy had to be considered, certainly on the occasions when there was little option. This was such an occasion. He didn't have any choice.

In favour of the strategy were two elements.

The first was that the information he had was far from confidential. What he did know wasn't much and any disclosure of what he'd managed to piece together would hardly breach any protocol. That was his reasoning.

In exchange, he might gain access to the senator. Increasingly, it had become obvious that he, above all in this story, knew how the pieces fitted together. He might not know the entire picture but it was a damn good bet.

McCabe couldn't progress unless he spoke to the senator. His sources told him that the congressman was in George Washington University Hospital, under police guard. Lieutenant

Kovarik would be taking no chances in that regard. That meant a horse-trade with Kovarik.

The second element in favour of the strategy was Kovarik himself. The policeman hated and distrusted the Press. That was a given. But the detective was trustworthy and his word had some currency. He would be uncomfortable with an arrangement with a journalist but he was a pragmatist with whom McCabe had done business before. They both realised that the other had useful information. It couldn't really be described as a swap, more a sharing.

The full picture would then emerge; that was the hope. He would give it a try.

In the houseboat, McCabe had just finished breakfast. He stared at his cell phone for another few minutes then checked his computer news-files to see if there had been any updates. He pressed the button for his contacts directory, scrolled down to Kovarik and pressed the button. It took more than half a dozen rings before he heard the familiar response. 'Kovarik,' the voice responded, almost deadpan.

An hour later he was in the hospital, outside the senator's room, being searched by a uniformed policeman while another looked on. About ten feet away Kovarik nodded with approval.

'Was that really necessary,' asked McCabe, a little annoyed. 'Don't you think that's a bit theatrical? You don't honestly believe I'm here to try and kill the senator, do you?'

'If I thought that, you wouldn't be here,' said Kovarik with a chuckle. 'Anyway, you're the man who claims he doesn't want

257

any favours, any special treatment; isn't that true? We search everybody.'

McCabe could see the detective was having fun at his expense again.

'I cleared it with the senator, otherwise it wasn't a goer,' said Kovarik.

'Is this going to be a waste of my time?' asked McCabe, sounding as if he was having second thoughts.

'How the hell should I know, McCabe. This was your idea, remember?'

The Lieutenant walked ahead, between two other uniformed police armed to the teeth, through the door then into the room.

The senator was sitting upright in the bed, looking surprisingly well. He looked a little pale but otherwise in good shape.

McCabe was relieved, if not elated. He had visions of trying to conduct an interview with someone on his back, half comatose and heavily drugged.

The senator looked alert, smiled and extended his right hand in greeting. 'Mr. McCabe. Believe it or not, I was going to contact you.'

McCabe didn't like the opening; *believe or not.* Just as well he didn't have to list the lies he'd been told after that hackneyed phrase. The game of the senator's spy-world was innuendo. McCabe had learned that only half the business was intelligence gathering. The other was speculation. What you didn't know was invented. He was trying not to prejudge the outcome or prematurely evaluate the credence of what he was about to be

258

told. He smiled, hoping he was not going to be served a dish full of caveats and ambiguities; the standard fare of Capitol Hill.

McCabe pulled up the empty chair beside the senator.

Kovarik stood by its side. He was staying out of this part of the show.

'What do you know already?' asked the congressman.

McCabe wasn't over-keen on that opening gambit either.

'I know what you've agreed with the Lieutenant. I'm party to it also. I just wanted to know where to start.'

McCabe looked more relaxed now. 'It's difficult to know where to start. I suppose I'll tell you my story, as it unfolded. It's with the gaps and the timing where I'm hoping you'll help.'

'I remember what you told me when we first met. And I'm sorry if I was a little guarded then. Perhaps we should start again then we won't leave anything out,' suggested the senator.

McCabe nodded and pulled his chair a little closer. 'If you recall I got involved through the death of a very close friend in Scotland. It was an accident apparently but the British Security services took a keen interest. That alerted me immediately.'

'Yes, the British have a stake in this.'

'When I returned to Washington, my houseboat was burgled then ransacked. I thought they were looking for some papers I'd been given in Scotland.'

'Perhaps,' commented the Congressman. 'I don't have any knowledge of that. But is it this you brought from the UK?' he asked, opening a file on his lap and producing a listing.

259

McCabe recognised it immediately. He didn't know if it was the same he'd asked Walker to interpret but it looked similar.

'I can fill in this gap for you which might make things clearer.' McCabe pulled out a pen and a small notebook from his inside pocket. He gestured to the senator, as if asking permission. 'Do you mind?'

'Not at all; use the information but please don't quote me.' McCabe nodded then made a few notes.

'Almost as a matter of routine, the late Professor Draper whom you spoke to would monitor the movement of nuclear waste across the globe. His interest was as a physicist, my interest was national security.' The senator stopped and turned over a few of the pages in his file. He looked up at McCabe again.

'I'm beginning to see,' said McCabe suddenly. 'There are other parts to this story. Am I right?'

McCabe flipped to one of the pages in his notebook and read part of the email Walker had sent him. 'This whole story centres round a consignment taken by the Americans out of a Physics Research complex in Soviet Georgia.'

The senator seemed unsure how to proceed, visibly surprised by what McCabe already knew. 'As was, Mr. McCabe. Soviet Georgia, as was,' he repeated.

'And it was taken to Dounreay, in Scotland,' said McCabe watching the senator's every move.

The congressman was looking increasingly nervous.

'Let me continue, sir, and when I get it wrong stop me,' added McCabe scribbling a few more notes into his book. 'But something went wrong with the transport, or there was something amiss in the consignment?' He waited for a response. The senator just stared ahead.

McCabe looked at Kovarik who was staring at the congressman too.

McCabe was ready to repeat the question.

The congressman still looked as if he was fighting some inner battle. Eventually, something emerged. 'This is classified but hell; it has to come out sometime. Keeping it secret caused all this trouble. It was a complete fuck up.' He stopped and went into silent mode again, staring straight ahead.

McCabe waited in the silence.

Kovarik was getting impatient.

The congressman fingered his file nervously, rifled through the papers again until he found the one he wanted, read it slowly then seemed to sigh in resignation.

'The region was totally unstable. Because of the role they'd played, the Soviets were on the back foot. So, the Americans insisted they take charge. Reluctantly, the Russians agreed. The US would take the consignment; 5 kilograms of lethal uranium suitable for a nuclear weapon, and place it in a remote and secure environment to prevent terrorists getting their hands on it.'

'But it wasn't that simple, was it?' commented McCabe.

'Yes, Mr. McCabe. It wasn't that simple. These things never are.' The congressman clammed up for a moment then began to speak again. 'There was still a lot of opposition in Moscow.'

McCabe interrupted. He'd been consulting his own notes again. 'But one of the terrorist groups got there first before the Americans could ship it out?'

The senator smiled. Now he knew why the journalist had his reputation. He stared ahead again, entranced, transported into another time. 'It was meant to embarrass the US or worse. Who knows? But the fuel was gone and the guards killed. The situation with the Russians was even more untenable.'

'Why not come clean and tell the Russians?' asked McCabe.

'We couldn't. The political future, or indeed the lives, of those that had supported us would be at risk. Somebody had betrayed us. We weren't sure what game we were playing then. They wouldn't believe us anyway. They already thought we had other plans.' The senator's face lost most of its colour. 'It was my problem to solve.'

McCabe was still writing. 'So you fabricated the whole thing. You pretended you had it and had taken it to Dounreay; hence all the publicity surrounding its supposed secret arrival?'

'The British even contrived a ban on its further transportation to North Carolina, to make the story sound authentic,' added the senator.

'That got widespread publicity too. All meant to convince the Russians that you had it and had taken it to Scotland?' commented McCabe.

The senator looked tired and pulled out the original listing. 'The game was up when the professor noticed the discrepancy in the weight and arrival timing of the consignment delivered to Dounreay.'

McCabe flipped to another page in his notebook. 'And they had a spillage too which wasn't even radioactive. That convinced the Russians there was something going on.'

'We think that's what triggered an interest from your friend Andy Gallagher.'

The congressman sighed again. 'So, the Russians thought they'd been double-crossed. We completely sealed off the plant in Georgia to contain further rumours but the damage had been done. As I said, it was a complete fuck up. By this time, the Russians were convinced we had duped them and we were using the consignment for our own purposes. With the wisdom of hindsight, we should have come clean but we would have been labelled as incompetent and not to be trusted guarding such a payload again. And, as I said, our political allies in Moscow would be no more.' The senator slid back on the bed and rested his head on the pillow. 'That was the story your friend was pursuing. He wasn't far from proving it either.'

'The attacks on you and the professor?' asked McCabe.

'We now know it was a Russian agent called Solokov.' The senator shook his head, yet again. His voice began to break with emotion. 'So many innocent people killed with this stupid deception. There was also a young researcher, who had previously been a student of the professor. By coincidence he worked for the CIA. He noticed the discrepancies in the consignment data too and went to see the professor.'

'But why kill him? He was no threat.' quizzed McCabe.

The senator looked exhausted. 'It's curious how circumstances and timing can change the very nature of things. Events can generate their own momentum.' He turned to Kovarik. 'Did you discover anything when you searched Aiden Johns' house?'

'No,' said the detective. 'We found nothing that gave us a clue to why he was targeted.'

The congressman leaned forward in his bed. 'My sources at the Agency, and they are fairly reliable, checked his office and his recent computer searches. They believe he knew about Solokov's arrival in the US. One of Johns' daily chores was to check a database that would have shown the Russian's arrival at Dulles.'

'And?' prompted McCabe.

'It's pure guesswork but fairly sound. They believe his timing was unfortunate. The researcher ran into Solokov in the Georgetown campus and recognised him from a photo on the database,' added the congressman. 'They believe the Russian sensed this, and followed him which resulted in his death.'

'He was killed for that?' asked Kovarik.

'Solokov was a trained assassin who took no chances. He wouldn't have thought twice about killing the researcher,' added the senator, now sounding very weak. 'Johns had probably just left the professor's office and caught a glimpse of the Russian.'

'Then what?'

'The Agency's conclusion is that Professor Draper was murdered by the Russian, probably shortly before. Solokov wanted to know where the consignment had gone and was convinced Draper would know. Then he went after Johns who was still sitting in his car.' The congressman now looked exhausted. 'The Russian was found dead by the DC police. Lieutenant Kovarik will brief you with the details.'

'I think that is enough,' said a young doctor who'd just entered the room. 'Time to rest senator; thank you gentlemen, that's definitely enough for today'.

CHAPTER 34

The coffee shop near the police headquarters, called Nu Deli, was Kovarik's favourite.

McCabe ordered two plain coffees at the counter and carried them to the seats in the corner by the far window.

'Well, was it worthwhile?' asked McCabe. 'I mean your interview with Forsyth. He was a little vague in some detail but much more forthcoming than I expected.'

'He was trying to make sure he didn't get blamed for anything,' commented Kovarik.

'I know that Lieutenant. I wasn't born yesterday. I have had some dealings with the likes of Forsyth before now.'

'I guess you got more out of it than I did?' added the detective.

'Why?' asked McCabe, sipping his hot coffee carefully.

The place was just emptying, after their usual busy lunchtime. A few diehards who could have been students, techies or both occupied the remaining tables, tapping away on their laptops or i-pads.

Kovarik watched them for a moment then turned his attention to his coffee. He took a large and grateful mouthful. 'I needed that. I'm not too keen on hospitals.'

'You were saying, I got more out of it than you did,' repeated McCabe.

Kovarik took another mouthful. 'Good coffee this,' he said, giving his cup an admiring glance. 'He used to run a little stall two blocks from here.'

'Who?'

'The Asian who owns this place,' said the detective looking round. 'Now he owns about six of these.'

'Perhaps we're in the wrong business?' laughed McCabe.

'You wouldn't do anything else, McCabe. I can't see you behind a counter serving coffee. What would you do with all your rebellious spirit?'

McCabe wasn't sure if it was meant as a serious comment. He chose to ignore it. 'What did you want out of it? What didn't you get?'

'You got your story; you're satisfied. I've still three murders to solve.'

'Haven't you solved at least two?'

The detective continued to sip but said nothing for a moment. In his time in Washington, the political side of the city never ceased to surprise and sicken him in equal proportions, and how common sense seemed to be replaced by silly games. 'Can I now assume that the Russians or at least Solokov killed the professor and Aiden Johns? It was pretty crude and stupid, if he did. I would like more explanation, more detail. But I guess they would plead *National Security*. However, since I'm not building a case that is lawyer-proof, it probably doesn't matter now anyway?' Kovarik sounded unhappy.

McCabe tried to be positive. 'You did get the motives from the senator's story. The Russians were convinced that the consignment hadn't been delivered to Dounreay. They wanted to find out where it was. Solokov tried to get the information from Draper but didn't succeed. His heavy-handed style turned into murder. Then he had a go at the senator.'

'You believe him?' asked the detective, sounding cynical.

McCabe thought for a moment. 'I think I do.' He said nothing for a moment. 'But I would have liked more explanation on how Johns knew about Solokov's arrival. I suppose it was one of those unofficial, if not unconstitutional, databases that would get privacy zealots into a rage?'

'There's another story for you, McCabe' said the detective. There was almost a hint of laughter in his voice. 'But what of Solokov? He is the third murder victim. There wasn't much insight from the senator into that killing. Was there?'

McCabe nodded slowly. 'I don't suppose,' he said cautiously, sensing the detective had something on his mind. 'He gave me the impression you knew the details.'

'You see, it gets a little messy there,' said Kovarik, finishing his coffee and looking instinctively towards the counter. 'Do you want another? he asked quickly. Before McCabe could answer Kovarik was on his feet, had gone, reordered then returned.

'Tell me about Hanya Smolka,' the detective said bluntly as soon as he sat down. 'You haven't given me much. What about your side of our bargain?'

McCabe was taken by surprise. 'What has she got to do with this?'

'That's what I intend to find out,' said Kovarik testing the temperature of the coffee carefully with a cautious sip. He nodded his approval. 'Not too hot. It tastes good as well. Sometimes the second cup is never as good as the first.'

'I've heard it said,' commented McCabe, humouring the detective. 'What's Hanya Smolka got to do with this?' he asked again.

The Lieutenant stirred the cup then took a drink.

McCabe sensed the detective was playing games. He wasn't sure of the game but it looked as if Hanya Smolka was one of the pieces. He didn't like the feeling and was uncomfortable.

'She visited the hospital and tried to see Forsyth. Apparently, she got spooked by a young doctor and the patrolmen I'd left there.'

'I'm not sure what you're driving at Lieutenant.'

Kovarik ignored the remark. 'My interest is in Solokov. Why he was brought over here, and by whom, may have some bearing on who killed him. I ask you again. Tell me about Hanya Smolka.'

McCabe was in a corner. The detective was not a man to bullshit. If she was in any trouble, she would be in it deeper if he told Kovarik any lies. The astute policemen would rumble him in seconds and the results would be fairly predictable. Again, he had no choice. So, he told Kovarik everything, from the first meeting in Moscow to her surprising appearance at his houseboat.

'And you had never seen her since Moscow.'

'I swear.'

'You, a man of the world, didn't think it a little surprising?'

Admitting being foolish to himself was one thing, trying to justify it to an incisive mind like Kovarik's was quite a different thing. The detective was almost as cynical as he was.

'Of course I knew she'd been assigned to keep tabs on me. I guess I was the stalking horse.'

'It didn't bother you?'

'You've seen her, would it you?' laughed McCabe. The opposite sex was a subject he'd never discussed with Kovarik.

He gathered that the policeman was happily married with no children but Kovarik never discussed or mentioned that part of his life.

Suddenly McCabe felt a little embarrassed at his comment. In retrospect, it sounded out of place. But he still didn't know where this conversation was going.

Kovarik sensed the confusion. He pulled a sheet of paper from inside his coat pocket, flattened it on the table in front of him, read it thoroughly then looked straight at McCabe.

'Perhaps in a moment you'll see the relevance of my questions.'

McCabe had no hint of what was coming.

'This is the forensic report on Colonel Nikita Solokov,' he said very slowly. 'Forgive me, if I tell you something you know already but I'll do this so that there is no ambiguity,' Kovarik

270

continued, sipping his coffee as he went. 'He was ex-army, then the KGB and now a trade attaché at large.'

'At large?'

'The CIA has a dossier on this guy the size of the DC telephone directory. The limited briefing they gave us, said that he's been linked to a number of killings around the globe.'

'I didn't think you rubbed shoulders with Agency folk?' said McCabe, trying to be witty.

The joke fell flat. The detective didn't respond to it but continued with his story. 'It means he's still an agent for their renamed state security, so we've been informed. He has quite a reputation as a tough guy, a man of last resort. Apparently, he's only brought in if there is a problem. Most who knew him considered him to be a psychopath at worst and at best an ace asshole.'

'Does it say all that in your report?' joked McCabe nodding towards the piece of paper in the detective's hand.

Kovarik managed a smile. 'No, that's from memory.' His eyes dropped to the paper again.

'We are convinced he killed the professor and Johns, the Agency's researcher. We're equally certain about the attack on the senator. The description we got from the shopkeeper in Georgetown sealed it. But we were too late to get him alive. He was shot not very long after, near the Russian Embassy.'

'By whom?'

The detective waved his paper in front of McCabe. 'That is where this comes in.'

'Why would it interest me? I have my story.'

'Well, perhaps you can help me?'

McCabe looked a little puzzled and stretched out to take the paper.

'Not for your consumption McCabe,' said Kovarik, pulling it away. 'There were two bullets in the shooting. I found one lodged in a garden wall behind the victim. And forensic found the other in the corpse.'

'Two shots, one on target,' commented McCabe.

'I still don't follow where I come into this.'

The detective continued, as if the journalist had said nothing.

'There were two different bullets and two different gunmen,' said Kovarik referring to the notes again. 'One gunman was an excellent shot. He fired the one shot that killed Solokov.'

'So? I still don't know what you want from me.'

'The other was fired by someone not commanding the same skill, not of the same calibre, if you'll forgive the pun.' Kovarik laughed at his joke.

McCabe didn't laugh. He didn't know where the conversation was going.

'I reckon that it was Hanya Smolka who fired the other shot,' said Kovarik quickly.

'What?'

'Yes, a real curiosity. It's forensic's guess that both were fired within seconds of each other, from different locations, the shooters totally unaware of each other. Solokov fell dead, job done.'

McCabe looked mystified. 'You're not serious?'

Again, Kovarik continued undeterred, refreshing his memory from another quick glance at the paper. 'Forensic were very thorough and managed to locate from where the bullets were fired.'

'What did they prove?'

'Absolutely nothing! But forensic science is not all there is to police-work.' Kovarik smiled with satisfaction. 'Well, science did come into its own here. Did you know that the Russian Sobranie cigarette is one of the oldest luxury tobacco brands in the world, originally handmade about 150 years ago? Its smokers are few but selective,' said Kovarik reading from his crib sheet. 'They burn to form a quite distinctive ash. There was plenty of it in evidence at the sharpshooter's location. Krupin, Hanya's boss and the head trade attaché at the Russian Embassy, chain-smokes Sobranies. Also, he was in the army and apparently is an excellent shot.'

'So your money is on him?'

'Undoubtedly; there was no love lost between them. Apparently he resented Solokov being brought in over him and he hated his crude tactics.'

'What now?'

'I'll pass the details on and the politicos can deal with him. But he's got diplomatic immunity.'

'And what about the other....' McCabe began to ask cautiously.

Kovarik folded up the paper and slid it back into his inside pocket. 'That's a difficult one. I wanted your input there.

Solokov was a complete bastard to most of those who ever knew him, particularly his wife, now separated if not divorced; we're not sure which one. But she hated him with a vengeance and with good reason.'

'Why are you telling me this?' persisted McCabe.

'He was the abusive husband par excellence, we are informed. Some claim his extensive combat was to blame. That doesn't concern me. But there is something that does.'

McCabe felt a cold chill down the back of his neck. He guessed what Kovarik was about to say.

'Opportunity and motive, usually that's all we need to act. In this case it's a little more difficult.' Kovarik hesitated for a moment. 'You see, the abused wife was Hanya Smolka.'

CHAPTER 35

It had taken McCabe several hours to write the story the way he wanted; a style that had both pace and gravitas. The senator had filled in some of the gaps but not all.

The story was a simple one, made complex by the political manoeuvrings, distrust and posturing of both the Russians and the Americans. In the wake of the turmoil in war-torn Soviet Georgia, the Americans had been trusted with transporting batches of radioactive uranium to a more secure location. It was quite a commitment by the Russians. The consignment was dangerous and in sufficient quantity to be considered a threat, capable of being used in a nuclear weapon by terrorists or equally threatening and ambitious enemies.

But the Americans had screwed up and before they had secured the consignment, a well organised third party had raided the Georgian complex, brutally killed the personnel, and stolen the nuclear fuel. Now, the US with the wisdom of hindsight, would have done something else.

They wouldn't or felt they couldn't admit they had messed up. Instead, they belatedly secured the Soviet nuclear location, ensuring no news filtered its way out if the complex. That was a gamble. But it was the least of their problems. They had decided to contrive a charade, as if nothing had happened, by delivering what appeared to be the consignment to Dounreay in Scotland, the venue sufficiently remote and away from prying eyes. The

US government's Public Relations machine was in full cry now, making sure that the local press was aware of the consignment's arrival. Later their allies, in British security, devised a story about the load's subsequent transportation to North Carolina. All this arranged press coverage was a vital part of the charade.

But keeping a lid on such an event requires favourable fortune. Instead, they had a number of strokes of bad luck. The first was a leak from the consignment when it arrived in Scotland. It suggested that there was something not right with the payload. The second was the interest it had provoked in a semi-retired Scots journalist, Andy Gallagher, who began to check on the other characteristics of the consignment. It didn't take the journalist long to discover that Professor Melvin Draper of Georgetown University, an authority on the movement of nuclear fuel around the globe, had written academic papers on terrorists acquiring nuclear fuel. Gallagher sought him out at a conference in Washington.

McCabe could only surmise what Gallagher had suspected. Did he really discover there had been a switch or was he just the tenacious professional, convinced that whatever the truth, there was a story. He guessed Gallagher had concluded that the Washington elite, with their fingers on the pulse of national security, would know the details. The next leap towards Senator Dorman Forsyth was inevitable.

By that time other interested parties had become involved, primarily the Russians. Solokov was the man at whose door the Americans were happy to lay the blame for the deaths of Draper and the poor unsuspecting CIA researcher Aiden Johns. The innocent youth knew something was wrong with the shipment which had arrived in Scotland and, just as Gallagher had done before him, sought counsel from the Georgetown professor. That visit was to cost him his life.

The Russian's death had allowed the authorities to close the book on the affair, except for Kovarik. He was still unsure how to proceed with that aspect of the case. McCabe knew the detective would have to tread carefully in those diplomatic waters but would never let it rest. Someone had been murdered on his patch, on his watch and, whatever the political implications, Kovarik would insist that the rules be followed. Undoubtedly, the detective considered Solokov to be a cretin and a piece of low-life but his job didn't include making moral judgements on murder victims. Knowing the Lieutenant as he did, McCabe guessed he would leave it to the judge, the jury or whatever God they worshipped to decide. But then there was Hanya Smolka.

According to the statement Forsyth gave from his hospital bed, based on reports from US intelligence he said, an outfit of special American forces had repossessed the consignment, so there was no threat to national security, if there ever had been. The congressman was reluctant to disclose that much, but he obviously was at pains to ensure the US Security Agencies and the politicos, who had sanctioned this risky and questionable strategy, didn't emerge discredited for what was clearly a monumental screw-up. McCabe would let the readers decide.

He read the story on the front page of the *Washington Post*. He spread it out on his desk on the houseboat and reread it several times. It had appeared verbatim in all the other major US and European papers. None of the newspapers objected to his conditions. He had insisted on a brief biog of the reporter whose by-line they prominently carried; Andy Gallagher. That was also part of the deal. He'd texted Irene Campbell. He hoped she was happy. He smiled, pleased with the result, at least this part. He looked at his watch. He had a plane to catch.

Dulles airport was busy as usual. McCabe checked his watch. Kovarik had pulled the appropriate strings to make things happen but he could only do so much. The rest, he said, was inevitable and out of his hands.

McCabe checked his watch again, just as Andrei Krupin emerged from the United Airlines First Class lounge, flanked by two very large plain clothed Immigration officers, who would not only escort him to the flight but accompany him all the way to Moscow. What reception awaited the Russian when he arrived would be in the hands of his political masters. The consignment debacle was not of his doing but the death of one of their favoured sons, Solokov, would need some explaining.

According to McCabe's sources, Kovarik had made it clear that it was Solokov who had been solely responsible for the deaths of the Georgetown professor and the CIA researcher. The attack on the senator had been left unresolved. In the end the Russians would have to come to their own conclusions regarding who was to blame for the mess which had strained the US diplomatic bonds to breaking point. Whether Krupin's recall to Moscow was cosmetic, and the theatrical extradition was simply for effect, no one knew. However, if he had one, McCabe wouldn't have put his pension on the Russian having a care-free future in Soviet employment.

But he hadn't come to Dulles to wish the Russian good luck. Five minutes later, Hanya Smolka, walked slowly out of the lounge, also flanked by two escorting officials. She looked pale and drawn.

Kovarik had insisted that she had played no part in the murders of the Americans or was in any way implicated in the attack on the senator. But it seemed to have little effect on the decision to extradite her too. Apparently, the US security agencies had been monitoring her for quite some time and had been unhappy about the ease with which she was able to assimilate into American life and report to her political masters. He suspected they would have loved to have recruited her as an agent but while she loved America, her heart belonged to mother Russia. So, she had to go.

Her reappearance in his life had brought so much back. How could he forget the glorious nights in the Russian capital so many years before when he'd barely made any impact on the world or the profession he loved? How could he ever forget his time with her then and but a few days ago? And now that he knew about Solokov, how could he separate the Russian's murder from the thoughts of her abusive marriage? He was having trouble with the thought of them together. Had they had more time together would she have been able to explain her feelings and what part she'd played in his death? Perhaps, it was better that he didn't know? Despite the bullet in the wall, which Kovarik had insisted came from her gun, those who pulled the power-strings had thought otherwise. If he ever came to write that part of the story, he wondered how he would paint her; the vengeful partner or the abused wife who'd struggled to build a new life?

So, was he here in the hope that the authorities would change their minds about her? He knew he was dreaming in that regard. A last glimpse of her was all he could expect. It was all he was likely to get.

 It was she who caught a glimpse of him first, standing about thirty yards away. As she looked straight at him, he felt his insides turn over. He would like to have sat her down to explain to her that this was none of his doing, that he'd tried his best, as had Kovarik, to make the outcome different. He would love to have told her that seeing her again had given him a slice of his youth back when he was single-minded and impetuous. He would have loved to put into words some of the feelings she was responsible for; those he had not felt since his marriage had ended in pain, all those years ago.

 He wondered too what was going through her mind as she stared back at him? Did she blame him for any of this outcome and did she regret ever having known him? As she stared, one of her escorts gave her a slight nudge and she moved forward, walking towards the aircraft. She turned towards him again, just before she boarded. She smiled and then waved. In a moment she was gone.

His throat muscles tightened. He could have screamed. He could have cried.

He stood for nearly half an hour and watched her plane taxi slowly to the runway, join an agonising line for take-off then disappear into the low clouds.

It was an hour before he got back to the marina. As he got out of the car he could see the Commodore racing towards him. Not today, he whispered to himself, please not today.

'It came by special delivery when you were out,' said the manager, handing him a box with his name and address written carefully in block capitals on the front.

McCabe thanked him then quickly made for his boat. He had a double Black Label as soon as he got in, drank it quickly and poured himself another. Over the years he had come through plenty of emotional trauma in his personal and professional life but what he'd just experienced was among the worst. He sat on the sofa then tackled the second Black Label. His phone pinged and he read a text from Scotland. *Thanks for everything. He would have been proud of the piece. It read as if he'd written it. Irene.*

He smiled, took a small sip of the remaining scotch then remembered the parcel. Unlike some packages he'd had which took forever to open, this one was little trouble. He pulled out the contents and laid it on the coffee table: a Russian Nesting

Doll. He examined the wrapping paper for signs of the sender; nothing.

He lifted off the first layer then carefully peeled off the others underneath. There were five in all. He didn't have to look for the sender's name anymore. Inside the last one was a card with small neat handwriting.

There's always a story within a story.
Hanya.

Printed in Great Britain
by Amazon